10/15

PULLED BACK AGAIN
BOOK THREE: THE FINAL FLAME

DANIELLE BANNISTER

For information about permission to reproduce selections from this novel, e-mail:
daniellebannisterbooks@gmail.com

Pulled Back Again: a novel about Twin Flames reconnecting.

Cover Design by: MJC Imageworks
mjcimageworks.com

ISBN-13: 978-1490930978
ISBN-10: 1490930973

BISAC: Fiction / Romance / Suspense

ACKNOWLEDGMENTS

First and foremost, I need to thank my beta readers: Kari Suderely (my first reader of anything I write), Kellee Fabre (who inspired what has become Chapter 20), Tawnya Peltonen, Jennifer LaFon, and Judith Frazee (who all suggested more insight into Hawk), Amy Miles, (for making me slow down the ride so you could breathe), Grace Davis (for making sure it worked with the teen group), Laura Anile (my indie author friend from down under who was never afraid to give it to me straight), and Jen Wendell (who inspired the character of Jenevra).

Without their suggestions, this book would still be only 30,000 words and missing its heart, so thank you, truly. You have no idea how important beta readers are to authors!

I also need to thank my editor, Cassie McCown over at Gathering Leaves Editing. Without her, you would be indulging in my misuse of the comma and semicolon.

And finally my kiddos, Tristan and Marina, who, reluctantly, allowed me the mass amounts of time needed in front of the screen so I could take this journey with you.

"Love is composed of a single soul inhabiting two bodies."

—Aristotle

PROLOGUE

June 15, 2031

Tobias

Gazing around Ma's living room covered in half-deflated balloons and colorful bits of torn-up pink and purple birthday paper, I can't help but smile. My baby is a year old today.

Looking at them now, mother and daughter, snuggled up close underneath the early summer sun, you'd never know their lives had been anything but perfect. Even the afternoon sun seems to agree with me as it pours into Ma's living room. Its warmth makes everything feel calm and perfect—my own little cocoon of happiness.

"Looks like someone had a good birthday," I whisper to Jada. She's sitting on Ma's trusty old blue-and-white-checkered couch beside me. Janelle's blond curls mirror the exact color of her mother's: sun-kissed fields of wheat.

Aside from those weeks in the NICU, she hasn't been sick a day since. People always marvel that she is the happiest baby they've ever seen, and she is.

Ma calls her an old soul. I can't help but agree. She just seems so at home in her brand new body. While other newborns tend to flounder with their new limbs,

Janelle is like a baby Buddha, reassuring us that all is right in the world now that she is here.

Smiling, I notice Janelle's hand is clasped tight around a lock of her mother's hair as she sleeps in her arms. She has on the cutest pink sundress peppered with white daisies. Her white ruffled cloth diaper pokes out from underneath, hugging her plump little legs.

She is just getting to the age where she can tell something is "different" about her mommy, though. Jada has been worrying about what effect the terrible scar lining the side of her face would have on her daughter. Although she won't talk about it, I know Jada is embarrassed by the permanent mark that runs from the edge of her left eye and along her jaw. When she found out she was pregnant, she convinced herself that no child would love a mother who looked as hideous as she thought she was.

It didn't matter how many times I told Jada how beautiful she was, in those first few months after Janelle was born, she worried that she would end up scaring her daughter. She thought of herself as a monster.

That's why we all held our breath the first time Janelle touched her mother's scar. Jada gasped, but her daughter's eyes lit up like a flame. She smiled and giggled, much to our relief. Since that day, it's Janelle's favorite spot to touch. She will sit in her mama's arms and run her finger up and down the length of her scar like a zipper. She hums a soft tune to herself as she does it, almost like she's trying to soothe away her mama's "boo-boo."

We never talk about the night Jada was injured—the night her father got drunk and slashed her face open with a broken vodka bottle. We don't talk about it simply because there are no words, no words to make the pain or the memories go away.

But that is all in the past. Her father is dead now and can't hurt her anymore. Only happiness lies ahead for us now.

"Your mother spoiled her," Jada says when I kiss Janelle's head.

"I heard that," Ma says, coming in from the kitchen with an empty trash bag in one hand and her old, beat-up camera dangling off the other. "Grammies are supposed to spoil their grandchildren. It's the law." She gives us her famous grin. Her newly dentured teeth shine bright against her black skin. Since Janelle was born, our days have been full of laughter. Some days my life seems too perfect, like I'm just waiting for that other shoe to drop.

Kari, our neighbor and close friend of the family, dropped off an enormous stuffed bear, labeled "Little Bear," earlier this morning. Little Bear is currently taking up half the couch. This kid is spoiled rotten.

Ma starts picking up the bits of paper on the ground. She's ever so careful not to crinkle the paper and wake her granddaughter as she places it in the bag. I shake my head and slide off the couch to help her. A train could run through here and Janelle wouldn't wake up. That girl sleeps like the dead.

I grab the bag from my mother's hand and take over the cleanup. Instead of sitting down to rest, like I'd intended her to do, she picks up her camera. It's the old digital kind. They don't even make them anymore. She refuses to go to the cardless models that sync up with your e-ports. She says she likes to print out the hard copies and frame them, in a *real* frame, like they used to in her day. I can only shake my head at her stubbornness only because I know I've got a good dose of it myself.

"Tobias, go sit with your family so I can take your picture," Ma says, looking over her glasses to find the "on" switch she can't seem to ever locate.

I put down the trash bag and sit beside Jada and drape my arm across her again. The two of them smell like freshly washed laundry that's been line-dried all morning. They smell like home.

A few snaps go off before Ma seems satisfied. She beams at us and places her hand over her heart before she walks over to her photo printer that sits on her writing desk to make her precious copies.

Jada chuckles softly beside me at my mother's antics. I nuzzle my nose into her hair and breathe in her healing energy. I haven't felt this alive in years, and it's all thanks to these two in my arms. I owe my life to my family. They make me stronger, so strong that I haven't even needed my inhaler for several months now. The doctors are baffled by my recovery, but I'm not. I know Jada and Janelle have cured me. I can't explain how, except that I just can feel it.

Across the room, the printer spits out her first picture. Ma coos over her handiwork, no doubt thinking about where she's going to hang this latest photo. Just about every inch of her house is covered with wall-to-wall picture frames. Soon she'll have to start adding on just to have more wall space to hang more pictures!

"Oh, he's gonna love this one," she whispers to the

photo, hugging it to her chest.

The sentence is so hushed that I almost don't register what she just said.

"Who is going to love it?" I sit up, suddenly tense.

Ma's shoulders freeze, just for a second, but it's just the sign I need to know she's hiding something.

"Um, no one, honey." She turns quickly away from me, stepping over a small pile of Janelle's gifts, and heads into the kitchen.

Something in my gut tells me to press her on this, so I unwrap myself from my girls and follow after her.

I push into the kitchen, temporarily blinded by the sun that pours into the room at this hour of the day. Once my eyes adjust to the change, though, I can tell she's going out of her way to avoid eye contact with me. She's scurrying around the kitchen for something, *anything,* to busy herself with. She starts picking up the paper plates from the kitchen table that have bits of angel food cake still on them. Pink frosting smudges across her dark fingers as she piles them up in a leaning tower. Without looking up, she flies across the room and throws them in the trash, clearly not wanting to talk to me.

"Ma," I say as though I'm approaching a scared animal. "What are you not telling me? Who is going to love that picture?"

She puts her hands on her wide hips, the way she does when she feels like she's being attacked. The fabric of her shirt is pulled taught as her shoulders straighten themselves to full height of 5'4".

"Not that it's any of your business, but I'm giving this picture to Hawk. I've been writing to him this past year."

My mouth drops open, but no words come out. I think my brain has gone into shock.

She brushes past me to the sink and washes the pink off of her hands

"You what? Ma, how could you?" I stand there, awestruck, as she methodically dries her hands, as though gearing up for a fight. She has no idea how angry I am with her right now. Then again, how could she? She doesn't know the real Hawk. Jada never told Ma about how Hawk had taken advantage of her, or even that Hawk is actually Janelle's real father.

Ma still thinks of Hawk as the boy who used to be my best friend, the boy that grew up in her house, who she practically raised herself cause his folks were never around. She has no idea about the way he changed when he met Jada.

"Now don't get all upset," she begins. Her eyes don't meet mine, so I can tell she feels guilty about not telling me sooner. "I feel bad for him, Tobias." She drapes the towel over her shoulder. "No one goes to see him. Not even his parents." She raises her hand to stop me from talking. "Now, I know that he killed Jada's father," she whispers so Jada won't hear, "but you and I both know that he only did that to protect her." She shakes her head sadly. "If he hadn't stepped in, Jada's father may have killed her."

I bite my tongue. I want to tell her so bad about just how brutally Jada's father was slaughtered at Hawk's hands, but I don't. It's not an image I want to replay in my head and I know it wouldn't change what Ma has already done.

Ma places her hand on my shoulder.

"Someone needs to let that boy know that he hasn't been forgotten about. And if his best friend won't trouble himself to even write to him, then I will." She pushes past me again, this time to grab a broom from the closet.

My heart thrums in my chest at what I'm about to ask.

"Ma, does Hawk know about Janelle?"

She looks at me as if I've grown a second head.

"Well, of course he does! Like I'm not gonna brag about my beautiful grand-baby! He's always asking about her, too. I send him pictures of you all every week. And don't you sass me about it. That boy ain't got nothing to look forward to locked away in that cell." Her eyes tear up and I just now realize how much his being in prison has affected her. He was like a son to her. A healthy son. "Tobias, he says he just lives for the pictures of little Janelle."

Of course he does.

Ma seems blind to the fact that her granddaughter has the *exact* same unique pale-blue eye color as Hawk. I don't know how it's never dawned on her that *he* is Janelle's father and not me. But you can bet your ass Hawk has it figured out.

I've been praying every day for Janelle's eyes to change color. Her pediatrician tells us coloring like hers usually darkens after the first few years, but now that Hawk has seen her coloring, we'll never be able to pawn Janelle off as mine.

I have no doubt that he'll come for his daughter. Maybe for Jada, too, and that is something I can't allow.

I'm lost in a million worst case scenarios as Ma gives my shoulders a squeeze before she leaves me in the kitchen, completely unaware of the danger she's just put us all in.

There is only one choice now. We have to run. Before he gets out of prison and tracks us all down.

CHAPTER ONE

Jada

Janelle stirs a bit in my arms when her papa goes into the kitchen, but she doesn't wake up. I watch his lean frame slip into the kitchen, his dark curls contained only by his short haircut. I absolutely adore that man. I never thought a love like ours would be possible. Of course, I'd never believed in Twin Flames before I met Tobias, either. Every hair on my body pulls me to be near him, even after all this time. It's taken quite a bit of discipline on both of our parts to keep our hands off of each other; it's not even a sexual need—well, not all the time—that I crave. It's just him. His touch is enough. Just being next to him, I know things are right with the world. Now that we're together, I know I would have waited an eternity to be with him. He is my other half. My Twin Flame.

How is it possible that I've also been blessed with Janelle? Tobias would have been more than enough to make me happy for the rest of my days, but now that she's here, I know complete and utter happiness.

I press her against my chest and feel her soft, silky skin. My lips touch her tufts of curls. I close my eyes and breathe in her strawberry-scented shampoo. My summer baby. It's hard for me to fathom that we almost lost her. Even though I carried her to term, she presented breach and she was deprived of oxygen for so long the doctors were afraid that even if she did make it, she'd be mentally impaired. The weeks spent in the NICU with test after test coming back with negative results didn't make the experience any less daunting.

I began to question my faith during those weeks. I kept asking myself why God was doing this to me. Hadn't I been punished enough? Hadn't living with the abusive father He'd given me earned me the right to have a healthy baby girl? Could He really be that cruel?

Of course, during that time, other dark thoughts started to creep back in. Secretly, I started wondering if God would take her away from me because He knew I was broken, not just on the outside with all my visible scars, but on the inside as well. After all, I had serious doubts about my ability to parent. It's not like I had a mother of my own to model from. How would I possibly have any idea what to do? My father wasn't exactly the best role model in the world. What if I lost my temper with her? Would I raise my hand to her as my father had done to me countless times? Had my father somehow taught me a way of parenting that couldn't be untaught?

I'll admit those were not my best moments. I was weak and scared. In fact, I never even told Tobias about my doubts. I didn't want to let him know that my father could still torment me, even after his death. I didn't mention it because he'd want to try and fix it, and there are some hurts that just can't be healed. Not even with time.

As bad as those weeks in the NICU were, though,

they weren't the worst thoughts I'd ever had. Those, Tobias *did* know about. He knew all about my most shameful memories. He listened, without judgment, as I told him of the years I spent carving out my name into my arm as a way of remembering that I wasn't my dead mother, a fact my father would often forget when he drank. For years, my father took his anger with God for claiming his wife during childbirth out on me. It didn't help matters that I looked just like her. Or, at least, he said I did in the moments before he'd hit me. Most days I'm glad he's dead, but then other days I wonder if he could have changed, if we could have become a real family.

Tobias is my family now. He's never thought badly of me, even when I told him about all of the times that I used to rely on pills to escape the torment of growing up in such a cruel house. He stuck with me through it all because he loved me. Me. Broken and unlovable me. Realizing that *one* truth made me realize God wasn't punishing me; instead, He had actually blessed me. After that revelation in the NICU, the docs told me that Janelle could go home. Things were finally looking up for me. I had paid my dues and now I was being rewarded for not taking the easy way out.

Smiling, I close my eyes in wonder. *How did I ever think I wouldn't be able to love her? Or that she couldn't love me?* I'd never been more wrong about anything. Between my daughter and Tobias, I've never felt so wanted and cherished in my life.

Just then, Tobias's mom rushes out of the kitchen and whispers that she's off to check the mail. I give her a small nod and hug my daughter just a bit tighter.

As she sleeps, Janelle's tiny fingers thread inside my long tendrils of hair, holding on to me even in her sleep. I'm probably breaking all the Mommy Rules by indulging her with constant cuddling, but her need is my need. I crave her touch as much as she seems to crave mine. The velvety soft skin of her irresistibly perfect cheek rests against my chest. Her face rises and falls with my breath, and I sigh, contented.

Tobias and I have even started talking about marriage. Well, "started" is an understatement. He's been asking me to marry him on an almost daily basis ever since that night in the hospital—the night I tried to kill myself. Not my proudest moment.

I was able to hold him off before Janelle was born because I told him I didn't want to walk down the aisle pregnant. It's not that I don't want to marry him, because I do. I adore him

I guess it's just a stupid romantically challenged part of me wants to wait until Janelle is old enough to not only share, but remember the event with us. I haven't told Tobias that though; I doubt he'd want to wait that long. Now that little Nellie is a year old, I'm sure he'll start asking me to marry him even more frequently, if that's even possible.

My life couldn't be more perfect, which secretly worries me. It seems like when people are the happiest, things start to slide downhill... at least that's how it always happens in books and movies.

I snuggle down and give Janelle another kiss on her head as Tobias walks back into the room. Something about his stance is off. His shoulders are tense and eyes are pinched together in worry. Worst of all, though, is the color of his face. It has practically drained out of him. He looks as though he's going to be sick.

"What's wrong?" I ask, instinctively latching on tighter to Janelle. She moves a bit under my protective grasp before she sticks her thumb in her mouth and begins sucking, drifting back quickly into her cake-induced coma.

Tobias's melted-chocolate eyes glaze over with what looks like fear. His breath seems labored and his fingers start to fidget against his thighs as he walks across the living room.

"Ma! Don't run away from me! We need to talk about this!" he shouts up the stairs.

"She's not there. She just left to check the mail." Tobias's eyebrows pinch together in anger. "You're scaring me, Tobias. What is it?"

He looks from me to Janelle, then back at me again. "He knows."

My breath deflates instantly, like I've been punched square in the gut. I don't need him to clarify those two words at all. The look on his face explains his meaning perfectly: *Hawk knows Janelle is his daughter.*

My pulse quickens as I try to calculate what this news actually means. For Tobias, it means everything. Hawk learning about Janelle is the one thing he's been dreading would happen since he found out I was pregnant. Hawk didn't know that he got me pregnant that night. I didn't tell him. It's horrible of me, but I didn't want him to be Janelle's father. Telling him might take that away. What if he wanted custody? I couldn't lose my daughter. So Tobias and I agreed not to tell him. Ever.

But now… now he must have put it together. From the look on his face, I can tell that he's terrified Hawk will take her away from us.

Tobias never wanted Hawk to find out about Janelle for completely separate reasons. He is convinced that Hawk is off his rocker. Tobias doesn't want Janelle anywhere near him. He's being irrational, of course.

I mean, yes, Hawk *did* get me pregnant, but to be fair, he didn't know I was high on my dad's meds and didn't realize what I was actually doing. So although what happened was awful, it's not like I could blame him for my own stupidity. And, *yes*, Hawk killed my father, but he was only trying to stop my dad's drunken abuse. I should be grateful to him. Hawk was sentenced with three years in prison just for making sure my own father didn't beat me to death. If anything, I think we owe Hawk a world of gratitude. But Tobias refuses to see it my way.

In fact, Hawk is a topic of constant discussion. It seems as though every month Tobias and I have the same conversation about moving out of New Hampshire. Tobias seems to think we need to hide from Hawk, and I keep convincing him that a move isn't necessary; after all, Hawk has made no threat to our family or made any indication that he has any interest in seeing us once he got out of prison. I'd be willing to wager that Hawk is actually pretty ticked at us. Neither one of us has been to see him since he was imprisoned. Tobias has put his foot down about it. It's been his one and only bargaining chip with me. We could stay in New Hampshire, as long as I didn't visit Hawk.

Ironically, there is a visiting prison center downtown

where we could go anytime we wanted and video chat with him. All we'd have to do is walk into town, check in, and they'll digitally arrange for an online meeting with him. It would be so easy, and yet, neither of us ever did. If I were Hawk, I'd be pissed at the people I thought were my friends.

I frown at Tobias's determined expression. He's not going to let the moving option go now. I don't *want* to move. I like it here. For the first time in my life, I actually feel like I belong somewhere. I have visions of Janelle running up the narrow kitchen back stairs to her bedroom. I can practically hear her feet thundering toward Tobias's old room—her room. This is her home. It's *my* home. It's been my home ever since his mom took me into her house with open arms when I got out of the hospital. I'm not about to let that go just because of Tobias's irrational paranoia!

"Let's talk about this calmly," I say, patting the cushion beside me. Tiny bits of dust dance in the slice of sunlight that comes in from the window behind me, but Tobias doesn't sit. Instead, he continues pacing across the floor, deep in thought.

"Tobias, you need to calm down—"

"Calm down? You expect me to stay calm now that he knows about Janelle?"

At the sound of her name, Janelle's tiny body shifts under me. I rub slow circles along her back, trying to keep her asleep.

"Keep your voice down," I scold. "So Hawk knows he has a daughter? Big deal? It's not like he's getting out of prison tomorrow, Tobias. We have time to talk about this like adults. For all we know, he might not want anything to do with us." Tobias stops pacing and looks up at me. "I mean, it's not like we've gone to visit him or anything. He may hate us for abandoning him like that." I don't mean to say that last part, but my guilt let it slip out. I *do* feel guilty about never visiting him. I know if the tables were turned, he would have been there every day to see us.

Tobias paces a few more times around the room before he finally comes to sit beside me. He laces his hand into mine and instantly I'm at ease. My whole world is complete when he touches me. It's a feeling I thought would fade away after the newness of him wore off, but it hasn't—not even a little. Each time he touches me is like a fire igniting inside my soul, a renewing, a rejoining. I feel whole when his hand is in mine, and when we're apart, my body mourns his loss.

"Jada, I know it's hard for you to think of Hawk as dangerous, but... you didn't see the things I did." Tobias looks away from me and to the floor, almost as though he regrets telling me that.

"What things?"

He scoots off the couch and kneels in front of me, squeezing my hand. He rubs the pad of his thumb in small circles against mine. I can tell he is struggling to form the words he's about to say.

"You haven't seen the way he's changed." He closes his eyes and shakes his head a bit, as though he's trying to rid his mind of an unpleasant thought. "He's not the kid I grew up with anymore, Jada. When he met you, he became—"

"Possessive." I finish for him.

Tobias nods at me.

"I remember." Although I never knew Hawk when they were younger, I do remember how Hawk treated me when we were alone. It was like he'd staked his claim on me. His hands and words were always firm, laced with malice. But aside from a few bruises along my arms from where he held me too tight, he never hurt me. After what my father had done to me, I could handle a few bruises. Tobias, on the other hand, doesn't have an aggressive bone in his body, so he's not the best judge of aggression when he sees it. I can't help but wonder, too, how much of what he feels toward Hawk —is just plain jealousy.

"Tobias, what did you see Hawk do that you're not telling me?" It's clear that he's struggling with how to phrase his words. He's always trying to protect me, afraid that I might break apart. I've had my share of hard times. When will he learn that I'm not made of glass?

He lets out a slow, measured breath before he speaks.

"That night—the night your father attacked you—"

I close my eyes, trying to shut out the memory, but it comes crashing into my mind anyway. Those thoughts are like a car crash; you know you shouldn't look, but you just can't seem to tear your eyes away. It's the smell of my father's breath infused with booze that hits me first, followed by the memory of his dry and chaffed eyes that glare at me with a murderous scowl. My father's hand is raised over his head, the broken bottle at the ready to come down against my flesh.

The traitorous flinch I give causes Tobias to stop speaking. A second later he's resting his head in my lap, trying to soothe me, and the memory dissolves into the past, where I try to lock it away.

"I'm sorry… I shouldn't have—"

"No. It's okay. He's dead. He can't hurt me anymore," I say with a smile I hope he believes.

I move my hand to caress Tobias's hair. He looks up at me and I peer into his delicious chocolate eyes.

"I want to understand why you have such a fear of him. Admittedly, Hawk was a bit on the rough side in what little time I knew him, but he certainly wasn't so terrible that I'd want to uproot our entire family just to get away from him!" I don't mean to raise my voice, but it pours out of me without control.

Janelle rubs her eyes in protest at hearing me get upset. I instantly regret my hostility.

"Hey, peanut," I coo, lifting her from my chest. Her tiny hands ball into fists as she stretches, her eyes squinting in the sunlight. I lift my shirt and bring her to my breast so she can nurse. When she's happily latched on and clutching a new clump of my hair, Tobias begins his argument anew.

"You have to understand," he whispers, "the Hawk I saw the night your dad died was different. You were unconscious so you didn't see the methodical way he ripped that arrow out of your father's chest to replace it with the broken bottle—he did it without even flinching, Jada." Tobias's face blanches just at the thought. "When Hawk turned back to look at me after, there was nothing there. His eyes were cold, menacing. Evil."

I bite my lip at the worry that has blanketed his face.

"It was the same look he gave me when I accused him of taking advantage of you in the woods. In the moment before he sucker punched me, his eyes did the same thing. They glazed over. He shifted into something—different. The Hawk I grew up with, the guy who used to stand up for me against bullies, had turned into a monster, and I was afraid of him."

Tobias rubs his face with his hands.

"Something changed in him the day he met you, Jada. I know you don't believe it, but I just know he's not going to feel any different once he gets out of prison. In fact, every fiber of my body tells me that he'll come after you."

Tobias takes my hand in his again. "That's why we have to move." His voice cracks. "Before he gets the chance to try and steal you away from me, Jada. Please. Do this for me, for our daughter."

Those last words land harder in my mind than expected. He knows I'd do anything for Janelle if I thought there were a real threat to her. *If.*

"Let me sleep on it, okay?"

His face breaks into his perfectly crooked smile. He thinks he's won the debate, but I'm not agreeing to anything. Not yet. Not until I talk with Hawk myself. This whole thing has been blown *way* out of proportion. I love my home and the life I have here in Webster. I don't want to move. For once, I finally feel comfortable in my own skin. The last thing I want to do is move to a whole new place where people would gawk and ask questions about how I got my scar. At least here everyone knows my story and keeps their snide remarks to themselves.

Apparently, it's time I prove to Tobias that Hawk is no real threat to us. This is just Tobias's jealousy coming through. It's time that I prove to him this is all one big misunderstanding.

CHAPTER TWO

Tobias

While Ma resumes cleaning up the living room, Jada heads upstairs to try and put Janelle down for the rest of her nap. Me? I head to the basement to find some luggage. She hasn't agreed to move—yet, but I want to be ready when she comes to her senses.

I flick on the lights and cautiously make my way down the narrow staircase, stepping over the broken board on the third step down. The earthy scent coming from our indoor potato garden fills the cool space. They are thriving nicely down here, away from the pesticides that killed off the others.

Looking around the room under the flickering florescent light, I start rummaging around for the red suitcases Ma used to use whenever she had to visit me in the hospital when I was younger. I remember hating the site of those bags. If she dragged those things up the stairs, it always meant I was getting sick and would be staying at the hospital for a long time. There was always the unspoken truth that I might check in one day and never check out. My lungs were that bad. Until, that is, I met Jada. She was with me when I suffered asthma attacks that should have killed me. I honestly believe because she was with me, I didn't die back then. I'd been waiting all these years for her. She is my miracle.

For the first few months Jada and I were together, Ma worried about my lungs, worried incessantly that my recovery was only temporary. As the days ticked by and I got stronger, she slowly started to believe that Jada may be the key. The day I stopped using my meds, she almost had a panic attack. A month later, she moved the red suitcases down to the basement, finally convinced that we wouldn't need them anymore. I got to hand it to her—she did a damn good job of hiding them. I can't find anything down here!

Every corner of the basement is piled high with junk. Trunks filled with Ma's clothes from her "skinny years." She'll never part with them because she swears she'll fit into them again. One whole corner of the basement is filled to the brim with my old baby clothes, many of them with their tags still attached. She adopted me later in life and had no other kids of her own and overestimated how many onesies a baby actually needs. She was saving them for Janelle, but of course when we found out she was a girl, Ma had to go and buy brand new sets, all in pink. Of course, she won't throw this batch away, just in case we decided to have more.

I kick a few old boxes crammed with stuff and labeled "yard sale" out of the way as I search. One of the boxes topples over and comes crashing to the concrete. The sound of broken glass confirms that whatever was inside didn't survive the fall. *Oops.*

I freeze for a second, waiting for Ma to come running to find out what broke, but she doesn't. Cursing, I start picking up the shards and I place them in an empty box at the base of the stairs. I'll bring it up with the suitcases, if I ever find them!

I'm not sure yet what we'll tell Ma. I highly doubt she'll wanna come with us. This place is her home. Then again, she may be willing, now that Janelle is here. Ma is just as smitten with her granddaughter as she had been with Hawk.

Hawk.

What do I tell Ma about Hawk? She'll never believe he'd be capable of harming any of us. Of course, she's never seen his darker side.

In the end, though, it won't matter what Ma thinks. I'm moving my family out of this town. I need to protect Jada. She's been through more than any one person should in a lifetime. It's my job to protect her in any way I can.

As I try to move a box full of hangers, it slips out of my grasp and comes crashing to the ground, the hangers tangling themselves into a plastic web of interlocking hooks. Annoyed, I bend over and start cramming them back to into the box. It's as I reach down to grab another load that I find them: three blood-red cases tucked under the bottom of the mountain. I shake my head. Only my mother wouldn't actually stack the cases inside one another the way they're supposed to be stored. Nope. She leaves them out so they can fill as much space as possible.

Grumbling, I start moving aside randomly filled boxes of junk, not paying any attention to where they land. When I finally grasp the cracked plastic handle, I give it a good yank. The smallest of the cases comes free from the pile.

I can't help but frown at the state it's in. Three corners of the case sport thick coatings of silver duct tape. A new crack along the front will need repair now as well. I'd forgotten how often they've been used. Stroking a thumb across the worn leather, I whisper that I just need one last trip out of them.

The middle case comes free without any effort; it looks a little better than the first. Yanking the largest one from its nesting spot however, I feel my lungs constrict a bit. *Weird.* They haven't felt tight in months. Guess I've pushed myself harder than I thought. I set the case down gently and sit on the edge of it, trying to slow down my breathing. The pain doesn't subside, though. In fact, it actually gets a little worse.

"Ma!" I yell, rubbing at my chest. "Can you toss down my inhaler?"

I wait, hunched over on the suitcase, for her feet to shuffle across living room and into the kitchen, but they don't come. She must not have heard me. Annoyed, I yell again. Still, no answer.

That's not like her. Ma's a worrywart. She's just in the living room. She would have heard me; the floorboards aren't that thick. Tilting my head up, I listen again. It's quiet. Too quiet.

Dropping the cases, I fly up the stairs faster than my lungs would like and immediately scan the kitchen. Ma's tea water sits blinking that it's ready yet still un-poured in its carafe. My already strained breath comes faster.

Spying the white medical kit on top of the fridge, I grab it, flip open the latches, and grab one of three inhalers tucked inside. I take a quick series of puffs before I pocket it and jog into the living room. It, too, is empty.

"Ma!" I shout again. "Jada?"

The only answer I get is a creak in the floorboards upstairs. My fists clench instinctively as I run up the stairs two at a time. At the top, I notice that the bathroom door is open and the lights are off. The light drip from the faucet thunders in my eardrums. Our room is down the hall, the door is slightly ajar, but it's Janelle's room that pulls me closer. A muted noise comes from behind her closed door. Shadows dance against the sun that pours out of her room from a crack at the bottom of the door. My eyes dart around for something to use in defense. The only thing there is our fake banana tree.

Slowly, I bend over and grab the base of it, ready to take down whoever is in my daughter's room. As I set my jaw, my muscles tense in anticipation. I bring my foot to the door and kick it open, ready for anything— except for what I see.

"Tobias Daniel Garret!" Ma shouts. She's sitting in the rocking chair and holding Janelle. Janelle, who is, of course, now crying. "What are you trying to do? Scare us both to death?"

My heart hammers in my chest as I lower the tree.

"Ma! What are you doing?" I rub my hand over my face, trying to wipe away the scene I created in my mind.

Ma frowns at me. "I was trying to get your daughter to finish her nap, but now *that* is out of the question." Janelle shrinks away when I try to hold her, clinging instead to the person who didn't just burst in acting like a maniac. "What has gotten into you, breaking down the door like that?"

"I thought—" I can't actually admit what I thought. She'd tell me I was being paranoid. And maybe I am. I can't seem to stop thinking about Hawk trying to hurt my family, even when he's still in prison.

"I thought Jada was putting her down?"

Ma's eyes drop to the ground. The chills I had in the basement return.

"Ma, where *is* Jada?"

She frowns at me and shifts Janelle to her other shoulder. "Tobias, I need you to calm down. You're upsetting your daughter." Ma plants a series of gentle kisses in her granddaughter's sea of curls. "Jada is a big girl. She can take care of herself."

"Ma," I say, my paranoia returning. "Where is she?" My feet plant themselves into the beige carpet, conveying with every pore that I'm not budging until she fesses up.

Ma stands up, glaring at me down her stubby nose. She rubs Janelle's back and rocks slowly from side to side. "She went to visit a friend."

A friend.

Bullshit.

The nausea bubbling up in the pit of my stomach tells me the truth. She's gone to see Hawk.

Jada

Peddling Tobias's bike toward the jail, I can't help but feel guilty about not telling him what I'm up to. But I know he'd just try to stop me and I wanted this silliness to be done with.

Convincing his mother to take care of Janelle while I went was a snap. She's been urging me to see Hawk for almost two years now. Even she agrees with me; Hawk is essentially harmless. He's just lonely and misunderstood. I know what that's like more than anyone.

By taking his bike, I've bought myself a nice window of time. It's currently the only transportation at the Garret house, so when Tobias finds out I left, it will take some finagling on his part to catch up with me.

I'm cordial with the mass of other bikers I pass. Cyclists far outnumber cars these days. The fuel crisis doesn't seem to be getting any better, forcing more and more people to take alternate transportation. I find it ironic how we've been forced by Mother Nature and her dried-up oil supplies into becoming greener.

I'm drenched in my own sweat by the time I make it into town. The summer sun showed me no mercy and the uphill journey didn't exactly help. Locking the bike up in one of the racks outside the viewing station, I take a few shaky steps toward the building. Now that I'm here, I'm not exactly sure what I'm supposed to do. Or say for that matter. I haven't seen him in so long—how will he react to seeing me? Will he be angry? Happy? Indifferent?

As I push open the door, the large cement walls

swallow me up from the burning daylight. I notice almost at once that the air inside is damp and thick—stale. It's like trying to breathe underwater. It's amazingly depressing. The bright-white overhead lights don't make matters any better. They are harsh against my eyes and yet flick just enough to drive even a sane person crazy.

"Can I help you?" A large man in dark brown uniform speaks to me from behind what I assume is a bulletproof glass window. In front of him is a series of flat screens that he seems to be monitoring. A camera from above his head captures my every move.

Clearing my throat, I step up to the small series of holes that have been carved out of the glass.

"I'm here to video chat with Hawk Sanders." I'm surprised by how tiny my voice sounds. The words are almost gobbled up in the dark corners of the room.

The guard looks down at the screens for a moment, clicking buttons, then back up at me.

"What's your name?"

"Um, I don't have an appointment or anything."

"I still need a name, miss."

"Oh, of course. I'm sorry. My name is Jada. Jada Williams. I'm a friend of his. We went to school with Hawk before..." I'm babbling now. I don't know why I'm so nervous.

A curious look spreads across the guard's face. "Oh yeah. I know you. I remember reading about you two in the papers. He's the one who killed your daddy, right?" He pushes out of his chair to look me over. Instinctively, I yank out my ponytail and hang my head a bit so my hair falls over most of the left side of my face and pull the sleeves down on my jacket. I may have come to terms with my cutting past, but other just ask questions.

"Um, yeah." Sometimes I forget our story was once front-page news.

The guard stares at me for a moment longer before he goes back to his screen. "It'll take me a few minutes to get him online. In the meantime, I can get you set up in the screening room."

I straighten myself up as he slides off his stool. After a moment, the guard opens the door to his left and ushers me inside where I'm sent through a series of metal detectors. Why I need to be checked for weapons since there are no actual prisoners in the building seems like overkill, but ever since the last terrorist attack, all federal buildings do it. I'm required to take off my earrings and the ring that holds Janelle's birthstone and place them in a bin that will remain outside the screening room.

Even the small jacket with zippers isn't allowed inside. Instinctively, I place my hand over the name etched into my flesh. It's a habit you get used to.

As I shiver against the cool air, the guard directs me to the eye scanner, which officially signs me in before he opens a second door leading to a wall of screens. Each monitor has two chairs placed in front of it with only the barest of space between each station.

There is no privacy with these visits at all. Every word, every glance will be monitored by no less than the guard behind me and the others that may live on Hawk's end of the screen. There's no telling how many others watch from the cameras circling above.

"Have a seat. I'll go and get him online for ya."

Gulping down my fears, I do as he says and grab the first yellow seat I find and wait for him to come online.

Hawk

The nurse hands me the plastic filled with a rainbow of today's attempt to quiet my mind.

Fools. We can't be silenced.

I pinch my eyes to try and shut out the incessant shouting that buzzes around inside my head. It usually works, or at least dulls the sound of it, but lately, it's been getting louder.

They were just whispers at first, tiny sounds that told me Jada was the one I'd been looking for. After meeting her, though… well, let's just say… it's getting harder to stop listening. So far I can shut him off, that one voice that dominates the others. He calls himself Seth. I've never met a Seth before, but this dude is scary. He tells me to do dark things, but I'm able to ignore him for the most part. As long as I can keep him at bay, I'm not crazy and don't need their pills to turn me into a compliant little puppet.

"Swallow," the nurse says, grabbing the next prisoner's pills. It's a dance we do twice a day. I swallow, then open my mouth and show the guard standing next to her my masked obedience.

He nods me down the line where the others await guarded escort back to their cells. Except for my cellmate, Ricardo, the rest of us are currently regurgitating our meds. The trick is to make a shallow swallow; it's not easy to do. Took me a couple months before I could get it right. Then, once they're up, all you have to do is fake a cough or a sneeze, pick your nose, something to get your hands to your face where you can spit the damn things out before they dissolve too much. They're no good on the street if the coating is too far spent. But I'm not worried about that. I'm not selling mine. At least not yet. I got nowhere to stash them. The others all have it in with Jed. He's a corrupt guard who takes a hell of a cut. I don't like Jed. He reminds me of my dad. I won't sell to him. It's not like I need the cash now anyway. When they release me, they'll send me home with either a stash or a script. Those I'll sell.

A lot of the guys don't understand why I go through the trouble of bringing them up if I'm not going to unload them, but they're missing the point: I won't be turned into a zombie just to make their lives easier. They may have control of my body, but I refuse to let them have control over my brain.

They can't control us. A dark voice bounces around in my head.

With the pills pressed firmly in my palm with the base of my thumb, I shuffle my way back to my cell with all the other neon-yellow suits.

As soon as I get in the cell, I toss the pills right into the urinal where they belong. After flushing, I crash onto my bed, faking the grogginess they're supposed to produce. Can't risk them finding out I'm not taking my meds now, can we?

While I "sleep," I make a hash mark along the drywall with the edge of my nail. 608 days. That's how long I've been here. Only 487 to go.

608 days of white walls and piss-colored suits. Washing dank cement floors and scrubbing the damn urinals.

Soon, we'll be out. Soon, we'll take back what was stolen from us!

I slam my head against the thin white mattress that lines my bottom bunk, trying to get the voices to stop.

"Shut up," I scream into the bed.

"I didn't say anything," Ricardo grunts. He scrapes a metal chair against the floor to write his precious damn letter on the dull stainless steel desk we share. Dude's in for manslaughter. Caught his wife with a neighbor. Ran the guy over with a car. He can't understand why his wife won't write back to him. Ricardo is a moron.

"Your damn chair is too loud." I curse, trying to cover for my slip. They can't know I hear the voices. They'll start injecting my meds, and then I really will be in hell. The meds make me forget her, and that I can't live with.

"Sorry, man." He returns to his incessant scribbling. He writes her every day. On cheep recycled paper. Not that he has a choice. It's not like they give us any screen time here.

"You know, maybe you should try to write to your lady," Ricardo says. "That is if she really exists." His last sentence is hushed, like he didn't intend for me to hear it. But my hearing is impeccable.

"What did you just say?" I measure the volume of my voice, masking my rage. *Masking Seth's rage.*

Ricardo turns away from his letter to look at me.

"Come on. We both know you're making her up,

man."

Propping myself up on my elbows, I glare back at him.

"Excuse me?"

"It's just, you've been here, what, two years? If she's real, how come she hasn't come to see you yet?"

In a second, I'm on my feet with my fist buried deep in the front of his shirt. His feet dangle in the air as I bring him to my eye level.

"Take it back," I spit at him as the voices in my head begin to stir, urging me to punish him.

Ricardo, wide-eyed and panicked, quickly retracts his statement and begins apologizing over and over.

"Don't ever talk about her again, do you hear me?" The words don't sound like mine, but they come from my lips. The voices in my head are now starting to come out of my mouth. I swallow down the anger that just overpowered me, and I lower him to the ground. It takes a great deal of effort to peel my fingers off his shirt.

"You're crazy, man," Ricardo says, pushing away from me once he's free.

I grind my teeth, refusing to believe him. I just lost my cool, that's all.

As Ricardo moves away from me I try to gain control of myself. I don't like it when I act like this, when *he* makes me act like this. I know it's just this place is making me nuts. Once I'm out, everything will go back to the way it was. I just need to make it a little while longer.

Backing away from Ricardo, I press my head against the cool bars.

Down the hall, I hear the sound of a guard approaching. I glare at Ricardo in warning for him to keep his mouth shut, then crash back onto my bed. I wait for the guard to make his count and move on, but the footsteps stop at our cell.

The loud clang of his electro-stick banging against the bars echoes inside our puny cell.

"Falconer. You've got a visitor."

My head whips up. I never get visitors. Even Ricardo raises his eyebrows in shock.

"Who is it?" I ask carefully.

The guard frowns at me. "Your grandma... I don't know. Some chick. Let's go."

Jada! Seth's voice throbs in my skull.

Finally, she's come.

Jada

Trembling, I fidget nervously again with the edge of my shirt. *Maybe this was a bad idea?* Maybe Tobias was right? Maybe I should go? I bite my lip, contemplating leaving, when the screen in front of me turns on. At first it's just an empty seat that I see, but behind it, I see the edge of barred walls. There seems to be a guard in the room; only his lower half and his gun is visible at this angle.

The faint sound of metal clanking against metal alerts me that a cell door is being opened. That sound is followed shortly after by one word that chills me to the core.

"Jada?" Hawk's strained voice reverberates inside my body; the sound of it is so disturbing that it makes my skin gooseflesh. The way he said my name—so filled with wonder, shock, and hope… it makes me feel sick to my stomach.

A moment later he yells out my name again, but this time his voice becomes more frantic. A man yells at him to calm down or he'll be brought back to his cell. The slight whimper he makes is laced with agony. I am overcome with guilt. I should have come to see him sooner. What sort of a friend am I?

Hawk's waist is all I see at first. A neon-yellow uniform to match the chair I sit in fills the screen. His wrists are bound with twist ties. I can see they're cutting into his flesh, either that or he's straining against the enclosure, because his skin bulges around the plastic. His palms are pressed together and his fingers are drumming anxiously against the others

When he finally emerges in front of the screen, my breath stops short. I barely recognize him. His once perfectly sun-kissed hair has been shorn down to uneven peach fuzz. The color of his skin has faded and paled. The strong jaw line he used to have now looks sunken in and weak. But it's his eyes that do me in— eyes that used to dance whenever he saw me are gone, replaced with an emotion I can't quite place.

"Jada!" The relief in his voice is palpable. I can't help but feel somehow responsible for what this past year has done to him. If I had been able to stand up to my father that night instead of just letting him hit me, Hawk would never have had to protect me. Because I was weak, Hawk is in prison.

I shake the dangerous thought away and try to focus my attention on Hawk, or rather what used to be Hawk. On the screen sits the shadow of the person who fathered my daughter.

Two guards on either side of him secure his shoulders with their hands, holding him down like an animal about to pounce. Hawk seems oblivious to the additional restraint placed on him as he leans in closer to the camera.

"I can't believe you're finally here," he whispers. The tenderness in his voice is jarring. His tries to reach a hand up to the screen, but it's batted down by one of the guards. Hawk hardly flinches at the abuse. I can relate. It's strange how your body can get used to maltreatment.

"I can't believe I'm here either," I say. My voice is shaking almost as much as my hands. My stomach churns with unease as his awestruck gaze rakes over me. Absently, I tuck a strand of my hair behind my ear. Of course, I realize a second too late the gesture is a mistake. His eyes shift from mine to the side of my face —my scar. This is the first time he's actually seen it since it happened. His face crumples and his nostrils flare as though he's angry.

"It's actually healed up quite a bit," I say, suddenly self-conscious. "I have one more reconstructive surgery to go through, but this is about as good as it's going to get." I bite the inside of my cheek, forcing the tears not to fall. *So much for getting over my vanity.*

As though sensing that talking about my scar is making me uncomfortable, he quickly shifts whatever emotion he'd been feeling and refocuses his eyes back to mine. His stare sends a shiver down my spine. A slow, deep smile spreads across his chapped lips.

"You're still the most beautiful girl I've ever laid eyes on."

My cheeks flush at his compliment. Though Tobias tells me I'm beautiful, it's still hard to hear, even from Hawk.

Hawk's smile disappears, and his eyes grow serious.

"What took you so long?" His question is so simple and honest that I don't know how to answer it.

"I—I wanted to come sooner, but..." *But Tobias thinks you're a lunatic.* I frown, unsure how to answer him.

"It's Tobias, isn't it?" He pushes himself back into his seat, shaking his head in apparent anger. "He wouldn't let you come see me, would he?"

"No," I say, trying to smooth the situation over. "It's just—it's been hard, with a newborn and all." As soon as I say this, I realize my slip up.

"How's my girl? Is she walking yet? Ms. G told me she's almost there. God, I can't wait to see her. Does she ask about me a lot? Did you bring any more pictures of her?"

His bombardment of questions about Janelle floors me. Surely Tobias's mother would have told him that I placed Tobias on Janelle's birth certificate as her father, right? He couldn't possibly think I was waiting for him to get out of jail so we could all live happily ever after, could he?

One look at the brightness in his eyes told me yes. Yes, he did believe I was waiting just for him.

I take a deep breath, trying to find the right way to

tell him. "Hawk, I don't feel comfortable talking about my daughter with you. I only came to see how *you* were doing."

Hawk stops smiling. His once-bright eyes narrow. His nostrils flare open as he slowly licks his lips.

"I have every right to know about *my* daughter, Jada." His words come out slowly as though he's being careful to not lose his cool under the firm grip of the guards.

Every bone in my body tells me I should deny his claim on Janelle—lie to him, convince him Tobias is her biological father. But I can't seem to do it. Somehow, I know he'd see through me.

"I think you lost the right to call her your daughter the moment you took advantage of me." The sentence is cruel and unfair, but he needs to know I don't want or need him in Janelle's life.

His face grows wild with anger. His teeth grit as he speaks. "Took advantage of you? I seem to recall you begging for it."

My mouth opens to speak, but he's right. I *did* beg for his affection. Well, my medicated mind did. Then again, my drugged brain also thought I was begging Tobias to sleep with me, so I hadn't been in the best frame of mind. Of course, Hawk didn't know I'd taken anything. I doubt he would believe me now if I told him the truth. Besides, the truth didn't change the facts. He was still technically Janelle's father.

For several minutes, I stare at him, unsure what I'm supposed to do. I just want to walk out, but he needs to know that Janelle isn't something he's going to get to claim when he gets out. On paper, Tobias is the father, but if Hawk made a claim of paternity, a DNA test would be run and confirm his parental rights. That was something I couldn't allow.

As I contemplate my options, Hawk's expression changes to one of what looks like secret understanding. "Of course…" he whispers, leaning in. A smile tugs at the corner of his eyes. "I get it now." He raises his finger to his lips in a *shh* motion. "Your secret's safe with me." He grins again.

"My secret? What secret? What are you talking about?" I grab on to the side of the chair, sapping it for support.

He leans back in his chair. "I know what you're trying to do, but you don't fool me."

I stand up, frustrated with his double talk, and cross my arms over my chest. "I don't know what you're talking about, Hawk, but I'm going to go now. This was a mistake."

I've had enough. He has sufficiently freaked me out. Maybe moving isn't such a bad idea after all…

Hawk keeps talking. "No, your mistake was not coming to see me sooner. But I forgive you. I know Tobias has kept you from coming. He doesn't want you to see me, does he? Bastard wants to claim you all for himself, but you're mine, Jada. You and our daughter. And when I get out of here, I'll come for you, for both of you. I'll keep you safe. I promise you that."

My eyes almost fall out of my head at his rant. *What is he talking about?*

"Keep me safe? From what? I'm not in any danger, Hawk. I'm happy with Tobias. Honest."

Hawk snarls Tobias's name. It makes my skin crawl.

The guard to his left cuffs him upside the head and tells him to calm down. Hawk tries to swallow down his anger, and it's terrifying. Once he's composed himself, he speaks again, but this time his tone is soft. Gentle. The way his demeanor changed so fast leaves me reeling.

"You don't have to lie to me, Jada. I know the truth." He cocks his head to the side and smiles. "Ms. G. told me everything."

My fingers dig into the back of the chair—furious that he's baiting me into staying longer, but I need to know what he's talking about. Slowly, I sink back to into the seat and I cross my arms over my chest, acting far more composed than I am.

"Ms. G. writes to me every week," he begins. I know this much already but don't interject; I have a feeling he's trying to get a rise out of me, so instead I stay quiet. "She hasn't come out and said it, but I know what Tobias is trying to do to you."

"What are you talking about? Tobias isn't doing anything to me!" I nearly shriek. I'm rapidly losing my patience with his head games.

Hawk tries to run his fingers through his shorn hair, but the ties won't allow him to get any satisfaction from the attempt. He throws his hands down onto his lap in frustration.

"He's brainwashed you, Jada. Can't you see that? Tobias has convinced you that I'm this terrible person for what I did to your father, but you know the truth. Don't you?" His crystal-clear blue eyes search mine. "I was protecting you, Jada. I killed that pathetic excuse for a human being for *you*—to protect you from being hurt by that monster ever again!" Hawk leaps out of his seat and rushes the screen, taking the guards by surprise.

In a flash, their shock sticks come off of their belts. The electronic zap against Hawk's neck causes his eyes to roll back in his head. His body goes limp in their arms as foam starts to form around the edges of his mouth. I shout at them to stop. Scream at the top of my lungs that they're hurting him, but the guards ignore me until Hawk drops down to the floor, motionless.

My heart races upon seeing his lifeless body.

"What did you do to him?" I shout to the guard on the screen. He doesn't answer. From behind me, the guard that let me in approaches.

"What did they do to him?" I hear the hysteria in my voice but can't control it. They're hurting him!

"He'll be all right, Miss. It's for his own safety. Don't worry. They zap that one all the time." He shakes his head. "Can't keep his cool. That kinda rage is dangerous." The guard sighs and places a hand on my shoulder. "Might be best if you didn't come back, if you don't mind me saying."

Shaking, I turn back to the screen in time to see Hawk's slack body being dragged out of the room by the guards, and then the screen goes blank.

"It's too bad. That kid used to be one hell of a football player."

I walk out of the building in a daze. The sun burns into my flesh, but I can't seem to get warm. A coldness has seeped deep into my veins that I know won't leave me any time soon.

Tobias is right. We do have to move—the sooner the

better. If we left now, we'd have a little over a year to disappear. Maybe by then, Hawk will have forgotten all about us.

CHAPTER THREE

One Year Later

Tobias

For days now I've been on edge. I pace the floors, constantly look out of the windows, and watch the news for some sign of his approach. I'm doing my best to hide it from Jada and Janelle, but it's almost impossible to camouflage. Hawk has been out of prison a full week now. *A week!* Even though I know we've done our best relocating, it's still nerve-wracking as hell to think he's out there—no doubt searching for us.

I don't know exactly what it was that changed Jada's mind about finally moving. All I know is that the day she snuck out to visit Hawk, she saw something. Something that made her understand why I was so adamant that we leave town. She refused to tell me exactly what happened, but it could only have been that she finally saw what Hawk had become. I hated that she had to witness for herself the monster he'd turned into, but it had been the only way to convince her that he'd changed.

It was Jada's idea to move to Canada. I wanted to go

someplace way more remote, but she rationalized that we needed to be in a place with free health care, just in case I got sick again. She also argued that we needed to live where there was a majority of white people so we'd blend in better.

In theory, we should be well hidden here... in theory. But there is nothing stopping Hawk from crossing the border if he gets whiff of our scent, a thought that haunts me every night. Of course, his crossing would be hard to do legally—another plus for Canada. Convicted US felons need special permissions from the minister himself before they can gain entry, and that process takes at least a year.

On the other hand, Canada's border is huge and has plenty of wooded coverage—Hawk's specialty. It's because of that little tidbit of information that I can't stop myself from constantly looking over my shoulder every time I step foot out of the door. I always feel like I'm being watched. Hawk was an impeccable hunter in high school. It's all he ever wanted to do. And tracking —that was his forte. He had a way of sniffing out his prey.

But we're here now, and settled in a place we can call home. I still can't believe Ma moved with us willingly. She loved the idea of spending her retirement with her granddaughter, even if it meant moving to another country. The only thing she hated was leaving Kari. The two of them got close before we moved.

Since then, I've kept up close contact with Kari back in New Hampshire. She was heartbroken when we decided to move, but there was no convincing her to come with us. Hawk wasn't gonna scare her out of her own home. She has her BB gun stuffed under her pillow, though, on the off chance he ever shows up. Like a BB gun would stop Hawk. I don't tell her that, though, because I don't want to worry her. According to Kari, she hasn't seen or heard about Hawk since his release. She thinks he's moved on. Time will tell.

I actually miss Kari. We got off on the wrong foot, but during Jada's pregnancy, Kari was a constant comfort to us both. Although she had no kids of her own, she fawned over Jada and soothed her fears about motherhood. For that, I owe Kari a great debt. Her kindness to us during that time won't soon be forgotten. She's also been keeping an eye out on the people renting Ma's place. She's been a real blessing to us.

She was actually the one thing we hated about moving. We wanted to scoop her up and drag her off too, like we were doing with Ma, but she was stubborn and wouldn't be swayed. Webster was her home, she said. She was going to live out her last days there. So it was with a heavy heart that we left a few months after Janelle's first birthday.

We've only been back to Webster once since we moved into Canada. Ma had requested to be buried in the Webster Cemetery in her will.

We were all devastated when she passed away unexpectedly in her sleep a few months ago. Well, everyone except for Janelle. She had whispered to me the night before Ma died that angels were coming for Grammy.

I hadn't thought anything of it at the time, but when I walked into Ma's room to bring in her morning tea, I knew she was gone. Janelle was cuddled up on a quilt

Kari had made us as a going-away gift. Janelle was holding her hand, whispering to her Grammy that she was going to love flying up in heaven.

All during her funeral, I was a mess. She had just retired and begun her role as a full-time grandmother, a role she never thought she'd get to play. She never thought she'd have children of her own, let alone grandchildren. I wasn't supposed to live long enough to give her any.

It was Janelle who got me through that terrible day. She held my hand and said, "Grammy is happy, Papa. Don't cry."

I can't fight the feeling that Janelle knows more than she should for a toddler. It's almost as if she can see things before they happen. It's kinda creepy sometimes.

"I'm off to work now," Jada says, sneaking a kiss from behind me. I jump, surprised that I didn't hear her come down the stairs. She unplugs her e-port from the charging dock on the kitchen counter and slides it into her bag. It's the latest model, the kind with the slide out screen and keyboard. It's half the size of her other one. They call it "The Bookmark" 'cause it's about the size of old-school bookmarks. I have the older version. No pull out screen. Nowhere near as cool, but I wanted Jada to have the best if she was the one working. She hates the thing, but she carries it with her whenever she leaves the house to put my mind at ease.

"No, don't go yet," I say, putting down my cereal spoon and pulling her into my arms. I nuzzle myself into her golden hair and breathe in her intoxicating scent. Her skin against mine burns its familiar heat straight into my heart—rejuvenating me. The weekend wasn't long enough with her. It never is. No amount of time will ever be enough. Ever.

My lips find hers automatically. We fit together perfectly, like two halves of a whole. I melt into her kiss, tangling my fingers into her hair, pulling her closer. I just want to hold her and never let her go. It hurts too much when I do.

"Mmmm," she purrs, pulling away a bit and licking her lips. She knows I love it when she does that, so I pull her in for another round.

"You're making it really hard to leave," she pants between kisses.

"Then don't," I counter, lifting an eyebrow.

She lets out a small sigh and pushes fully away from me. A frown brushes her soft-pink lips. "I'm not going to stay inside forever just because he's out of prison, you know."

Her words pierce me because she sees right through me. I *do* wish I could keep her hidden, safe in my arms. Is it so wrong that I want to keep her pressed against me forever and never leave these semi-safe walls? I struggle with this maddening desire every time she leaves, but the realist in me knows she's right. She needs to work. We need the money.

Since my doc won't sign my work permit until I've been asthma free for a year under his care, Jada has been the one forced to bring in all of our meager income. I have one more month before he'll sign it and then I'll be allowed to pitch in. Not that I don't love being a full-time dad, because I do, I just hate that I'm not able to do more for our family.

As it is, we live paycheck to paycheck. After Ma's

will went through probate, all that remained was a few thousand dollars, just enough to move us here. The sale of her estate ended up paying for my insane medical bills she'd put in her name. The rest just barely covered her funeral. It killed me selling her house to the bank, but they told me they would let me know if an offer was made on her house so I could try to buy it back, but so far, we've not been able to save anything up for it. It's not like we could ever move back into the house now that Hawk is out, but something about someone else living there makes me sick. That's *my* house.

Jada slumps her shoulders. She's upset with the situation I'm putting her in. I can't keep making her feel like she's trapped here. I need to let go and trust that everything will be okay.

"I'm sorry," I say, hugging her from behind. I feel her heart quicken at my touch. I love that I still have that effect on her. "I'm a jerk. Go. Scan books. Make money." I kiss the side of her face as it crinkles into a smile.

"I love you," she says.

"I love you more." I spin her around and kiss her gently on the nose.

"Give Janelle another hug for me when she wakes up, okay?" She frowns again. "I hate that she sleeps so late."

"She gets her night owl tendencies from you, you realize?" I counter.

She laughs at me. "I know."

I get one last kiss out of her before she heads for the door. "I'll see you tonight." She beams at me. "Indian night!"

"Extra curry!" I sing back as she closes the door. Janelle loves Indian food. A strange thing for a kid to like, but she loves it—the spicier the better. There's a lot about my daughter that amazes me; her distinct taste in food is only the surface of it. I'm sure most parents think their child is unique, but she just seems so much more mature than other children her age. Her sentences are almost complete the majority of the time, and her kindness to strangers is uncanny. And she never shows any fear. It's like she instinctively knows that everything is going to be okay.

Sighing, I walk over to our front door and slip the deadbolt in place, wishing I had my daughter's sense of optimism.

Jada

I put on a brave face as I leave the apartment. Tobias can't see the fear that dances there. He's worrying enough for the both of us. The last thing I want to do is give off any vibe to him or Janelle that anything is wrong.

Since the elevator is out, again, I take the steps two at a time, suddenly feeling the need to get some fresh air onto my skin. A cold sweat breaks out on my flesh every time I leave Tobias; it's like my body rebels against his departure. It's almost as though I'm afraid to leave him—afraid I won't come back. I can't help but wonder how many days will have to pass until this fear goes away? Will it ever? Or will I always be this on edge?

Grasping tightly to the railing, I make my way down the concrete stairs. When I get to the bottom, I rest my head against the coolness of the stone and take a few steadying breaths. After a moment, I enter the lobby and push open the front door and head outside.

I have to plant a smile on my face because I know Tobias will be looking out our window to see me cross the street and I need to keep up appearances until I hit the darkness of the subway stairs. If he even suspected I felt as worried as I am, he'd probably never let me leave the house again! As it is, it's taken him a good year to feel comfortable with me getting a full-time job. Of course, the fact that our bank account was getting smaller and smaller by the day may have something to do with it. We managed to live on next to nothing with my part-time job at McDonalds, but we just couldn't live off it any longer. Our bills were mounting. I had to find full-time work.

I am beyond grateful that I've been able to land my current job as an Archive Librarian Assistant for Dawson College. The job pays well considering I don't have an actual degree. I think the only reason I was chosen is because I was the only applicant who'd actually read a *bound* book before; and that was sort of a pretty critical part of the work. The job requires me to scan old bound texts into digital format so the information can be saved before the books are turned into toilet paper. It's me in a room filled with banker boxes of books and a scanner wand. Most people would probably hate the sort of isolation that comes with the job, but not me. To me, being in a room full of books is heaven. I'm lucky, too, that Dawson is still up and running. Many of the universities in the US and Canada declared bankruptcy after the Depression of 2022.

The hardest part of my day, ironically, is when I've scanned the last page of a book. It hurts me to put it down the recycle chute. Each time I do it, it feels like we're throwing away a piece of our history.

Every now and then, they'll tell me to keep a book after scanning. Those precious few are placed in the university's archive floor, but those are mostly dull historical journals. The vast majority of books I scan are what people used to call "mass market paperbacks." Apparently there used to be a time when literally thousands of copies of one book were printed in paper format. The very idea of it is unheard of with the paper shortage as it is now.

Sighing, I grab my first book of the day; I flip open the pages and take in the aged scent of the paper. It's almost like dusty vanilla and some spice I can never put my finger on. Deloris, the head librarian, claims it's nothing but dust motes and mold, but it's not. It's a beautiful smell. It makes me think of home, which makes no sense because I never had any books growing up.

Taking one last whiff of its heady brew, I flatten down the first tattered page of *Romeo & Juliet*. I click on the scanner and the red beam of light hums across the page. Content in my little corner of the world, I begin to scan the pages.

Hawk

Walking toward the house, my muscles flex. My hunt for Jada ends today. It was foolish for them to run.

We'll find them. We will always find them.

"Stop talking to me," I whisper as my feet crunch along the gravel.

My feet make no sound as I take to her stairs. She can't know I'm coming. I need to take her by surprise.

I turn the handle to her house. It's unlocked.

Fool!

Pushing the door open as softly as I can, I peek in through the crack. The living room appears deserted. She's here, though. I can smell her jasmine perfume.

A soft clink of a glass comes from my left. I smile. She's in the kitchen. With measured steps I make my way in to seek out my pray.

She sits at a table, her back to me. Never sit with your back to an entrance. That's survival 101. I lean casually against the wall and pick the dirt out from under my nails.

"Where is she, Kari?"

My voice startles her. She spills her tea all over herself. She looks up at me wide-eyed and pushes back from her table. Papers she'd been reading scatter around her; some float to the floor. Her face has lost all color. She's scared of me. Good. She should be.

"And don't lie, 'cause I'll know."

She opens her mouth to say something, but she can't seem to speak.

She knows where Jada is; look at the fear in her eyes. Seth laughs inside my head. He wants me to torture

Kari in order to pull out her secrets, but I rein him in. She'll tell us where Jada's hiding. If she knows what's good for her.

It's clear from Kari's expression she didn't think I'd show up here. She probably thought my parents would have picked me up and kept me on house arrest or something. Fat chance. No one came to get me. My folks wrote me off a long time ago, but I was kind of hoping Ms. G would've showed. Then again, her letters just stopped coming one day too. *They all leave you, Hawk. But not Jada. We'll make sure she stays with us forever.*

I shake my head to clear the fog Seth creates in my thinking.

"I asked you a question!" I take my anger with the voices out on Kari.

Her lips flounder, no doubt trying to spin some sort of lie. So far I've figured out she's not here in Webster. According to one of Ms. G's early letters, Jada's house was sold off shortly after I got imprisoned and now it looks as though Tobias's place is up on the market. They left no forwarding address, and they are nowhere to be found online. They've vanished, or think they have. And they've taken my daughter with them. That's why I'm here. Ms. G mentioned she was chummy with Kari, or at least she was at the time of her last letter to me. They had to tell someone where they'd gone, and Kari is the logical choice.

Kari's eyes dart around the room as though she's looking for something to hit me with.

I'd like to see her try. Seth laughs inside my mind.

I notice her focus lands on her kitchen table for a

fraction of a second before they flick back to me. She doesn't want me to notice something… but what?

Glancing down, I see it at once. Sitting on her table is a small box full of carefully folded papers. Paper just like the type Ricardo used to write on. They're letters.

My eyes flick back to Kari's. Her eyes widen, giving her away.

As I reach for one of the opened letters, Kari tries to stop me, but I'm far too fast for her. Snatching it away from her grasp, I read the first few lines. It's from Ms. G.

I wave the letter slowly back and forth in the air and smile. So they *have* been writing. Interesting.

Kari doesn't say a word, and her silence is all the conformation I need. Lifting the worn envelope from the table, I know it will have just what I need. The return address. Flipping it over confirms it: Montreal, Canada. *Got ya.*

I give Kari a small nod of thanks and back out of her dingy kitchen. My fingers curl against the folds of the letter. *We're coming, baby.*

It's as I'm opening the door that Seth yells at me to stop. Pausing with my hand on the doorknob, I listen.

"Pick up, pick up," Kari whispers. My hand slips off the door as I feel my mind shift.

Is she calling the cops on us?

As I creep forward, I hear Jada's voice in the background. My heart leaps, but it's only a recording.

"He knows where you are. Get out of there, now! Run!"

She's giving us away! Stop her!

I'm raging, my feet flying back into her kitchen.

Kari's eyes pop up from the e-port, terrified.

"Get out of my house, Hawk! Don't you come another step closer, do you hear me?"

Get the phone, he commands. Before she can even blink, I snatch it right out of her shaking hands.

I end the call by throwing her port across the room. It hits her refrigerator before it shatters into oblivion.

Grinding my teeth together, I push the rage down. As much as I want to hurt Kari for warning Jada of my arrival, I know I can't. I'd end up right back in prison. *You have a plan, Hawk. Don't screw it up. Stick to the plan and we'll get everything we're owed.*

Taking one last calming breath, I glare at Kari one final time before I push out of her kitchen, snatching her car keys that just happen to be dangling on a little hook by the door as I do.

Thanks for the ride, Kari. This will get us there so much faster.

"Me. It will get ME there so much faster," I hiss as I rev the engine. Of course, now that I have a car, crossing the border will be harder than going in through the woods like I planned. *It'll be easy to convince someone to drive the car over the border with the stash we have. Then we can sneak in the way we planned.*

"Argh! There is no we! Got it?" I shout in the car. My fingers dig into the steering wheel. "Get a grip, Hawk. I'm in control. Me. No one else." My words bounce off the fabric of the car but seem to have little effect on the beast bubbling inside me.

Rolling my shoulders, I hit the gas. Soon, Jada. Soon, this nightmare will all be over. We'll be together. Just as we were destined to be.

Jada

The first book of the day is scanned, and reluctantly, I slide the paperback down the disposal shoot. Such a waste.

I grab another collection of plays off the pile waiting to be scanned and crack open the cover: *Jekyll & Hyde*. I've just finished scanning the first act when my e-port goes off. I can't help but smile. It'll be Tobias checking to make sure I made it to work.

Putting the scanner down, I reach into my bag, pull out my e-port, and pop out the screen.

I frown when I see the message isn't from Tobias. It's from Kari. My heart always races when she messages me updates, even though every one has been benign so far.

I tell the message to play and her voice comes on at once.

"He knows where you are. Get out of there, now! Run!" I almost drop the e-port in panic, but Kari's voice continues with an intense level of terror that wasn't there a second ago. "Get out of my house, Hawk! Don't you come another step closer, do you hear me?"

The message stops abruptly, right along with my breath. The e-port slips out of my hand, its side screen slides back inside, like a turtle retreating into its shell.

He knows. Hawk knows where we are.

I feel my body slip out of my chair and sink down to the floor as well. The tremble begins in my hands and rockets its way down to the tips of my toes.

Not only did he know where we were, but he went after Kari! We'd put her in danger! While I try to suppress my nausea, my fingers fumble to reach my e-port. I ask it to "return call" and hold my breath, praying for Kari to pick up, but she never does.

Covered in sweat and trembling, I fumble with my e-port, trying to regain feeling in my fingers. I have to warn Tobias. We have to get out of here. Now.

That's when I notice the date on Kari's message. It's old. Two days old. I must not have checked my messages over the weekend—which means… he could already be here.

Doing the only thing I can do, I take what may have been Kari's last advice, and I run.

Tobias

The soft sucking sound of Janelle's thumb in her mouth fills the living room as I clean up her toys. The quality of the sound through her baby monitor is in Ultra-Def, so I can hear a pin drop even a floor away from her. It was an expensive purchase, but one we both insisted on. Okay, maybe I insisted more, but that's beside the point.

Janelle is *not* a morning person, much like her mother, so she's still sound asleep. She'll easily stay conked out until 9:30 or later if I let her. We're working on trying to regulate her to a normal routine, but she seems to have a mind of her own.

I smile thinking about how her little lip juts out in determination when we tell her it's time for bed. She has us both wrapped around her pinky and she knows it.

Since I'll have to wake her soon, I start pulling out eggs for pancakes. That girl loves her pancakes.

Bending over to grab the frying pan from the cupboard, I hear her little body starting to move around. I love watching her wake up, so I leave the pan on the stove top and tiptoe up to her room.

As I head up the stairs, my e-port goes off. It's Jada. Probably calling to say she made it to work safely. She knows I worry. I click on her message as my hand grabs Janelle's door. Only two words flick across the screen, but they chill me to the core.

"HE KNOWS!"

Instantly, my pulse begins to hammer against my skin as I throw open the door, suddenly faced with an overwhelming need to see my daughter.

Janelle's pale-blue eyes stare back at me before they crinkle into her famous smile.

"Papa!" She reaches up her arms for her morning hug. Letting out a breath of relief, I race over to pull her out of her bed and into a massive bear hug.

"Oh, pooh bear, you scared me." I bury my head deep inside her blond curls, pulling her tight against my chest. I do my best to hide my shaking limbs from her and hold her as hard as I can.

She giggles in my arms as she blows bubbles on my cheek, her morning ritual with me.

"I want cakes!" She beams, pulling out of my embrace before I'm ready to let her go.

"I know, baby girl. I just need to call Mommy really quick." I bring her to the bathroom where she does her morning business.

As fast as I can, I return Jada's call. She's already out

of the office and heading home. She plays me Kari's message and I want to rip her through the phone lines and drag her into my arms.

"I'll get us ready. You just get home," I tell her, pocketing the device.

Janelle comes out of the bathroom, rubbing her eyes. Her belly gives a loud grumble.

"I know you want cakes, honey, but first Papa needs to pack you up a little bag. We're gonna go on a trip!" I say in my best excited voice, hoping she doesn't pick up on the fear lining the edges.

I take her hand and walk her back into her bedroom. She stretches her tiny little body for a moment before she walks over to her pile of toys and yanks out her talking doll.

As the doll tells Janelle she "loves" her, I quickly open her closet and pull out her old diaper bag. I dump out the collection of cloth diapers stored inside and start shoving clothes into it.

"I wanna help!" Janelle says, clapping her hands, unaware that I'm not playing a game. Since I don't want to worry her, I let her put in her favorite toys (her doll, which is still talking, and her stuffed pink bunny.) She runs over to her dresser and takes off a picture frame of her Grammy. She gives the picture a quick kiss before she tucks it in the bag.

Satisfied, she takes my hand and I lead her into my room where she helps me pack things for Jada and me. I'm not even registering what I'm throwing in the overnight bag. There's no time for that. I have absolutely no idea where we'll go. I just know we can't stay here.

"All done?" Janelle asks me as I gather the bags from the bed. Her bright eyes look up at me expectantly.

"All done," I whisper, looking around the bedroom that had been her home.

"Yay, cakes now!" She giggles and takes off down the stairs.

I hurry after her, setting the bags by the door. Jada just messaged me again to say she'll be home in five minutes. It's not soon enough, but it will have to do.

Janelle, in the meantime, has crawled up to the table and grabbed herself a fork.

"Let's get you some breakfast before we leave, pooh bear."

I walk over to the stove and quickly start making her pancakes for the last time in the one place we thought we were safe. *Where will we go? How will we pay for it?*

"Papa?" Janelle asks me as I pour some batter onto the pan.

"Yes, baby girl?" A line of sweat drips down my back.

"Are we going to see Daddy soon?

Her question shocks me so much that I drop the spatula to the ground. Her tiny eyes peer into me, waiting for my answer.

"I'm your daddy," I whisper, turning to look her in the eye.

"No, you're my papa." She giggles. "I mean Daddy." She raises her tiny finger and points to the drawing she made yesterday that hangs on the fridge. Scribbles really, but she'd been so proud of it that we had to put it up.

She slides out of the chair and points to the blobs on her drawing. "Mama," she says, selecting a pink swirl. "Papa." She points to a single yellow line. "Daddy." she smiles, indicating the tall pale-blue squiggles.

Swallowing hard, I scoot down to her level and place my hand on the side of her face.

"Janelle, baby. Have you ever seen this man before?" I ask her, pointing at the blue lines.

She nods her head up and down.

My heart thunders in my chest. "Where?"

Janelle gives me a slight smile, then points to her head. "He was in here with Mama. Are we gonna see him, Papa?"

I open my mouth to speak, but the words fail me.

Not if I have anything to do with it.

CHAPTER FOUR

Jada

The Metro seems to take forever as I try to keep my pulse in check. I message Tobias every few minutes to let him know where I am. Each stop the train makes puts my mind a bit more at ease.

Tobias has already started packing. The faster we leave the better.

I've already began calculating where we'll go. Obviously, it'll have to be back into the States at least until we can get some money saved. We could push farther into Canada, but the weather in the winter might be too hard on Tobias's lungs if he ever got sick again.

There's about a thousand dollars in our account right now. Money that was going to go to this month's rent. I hate having to run out without paying the bill, but I have little choice now. I'll find a way to pay what's owed once we're safe again.

A million scenarios play out in my mind as the train brings me closer to Tobias. Do we go back to New Hampshire to check on Kari first? Or is that just what Hawk wants us to do? Maybe he's not here in Canada at all. Maybe the whole thing was a setup so we'd go straight to Kari and him.

We couldn't risk it. I hate not knowing if Kari is safe or not, but I've already called the police and left an anonymous tip to check on a burglary at her house. I didn't dare leave my name; I'm too riddled with paranoia to even trust the police. All I can think about right now is running.

The air-brakes squeal. My stop is up next. I just need to walk two blocks. Then I can sink into Tobias's arms and breathe deeply again. As long as I'm with him, I can handle anything.

People bump against me as I fight against the grain to make it up the stairs. I'm elbowed no less than three times before I can escape into the tunnel that leads upstairs.

With every step I take closer to the apartment, I begin to feel a bit safer. I'm on edge though, so I look up at every face I pass just long enough to make sure they aren't Hawk. They're all smiling or chatting on their e-ports—all oblivious to the fact that I'm having a nervous breakdown inside my own skin.

As I turn the corner, I see our apartment building. The worn red brick calls me home like a beacon. From here I can make out our outdoor patio. Our two bright-red plastic chairs sit side by side with a tiny pink one wedged in the center. Janelle's pushbike is outside, which tells me she's probably still asleep. She loves to ride that thing. The sun hasn't made it over the building yet, so it covers the entrance in a gloomy sort of shadow. The trees that mirror the brick pillars make it even darker. Despite the eeriness of the entrance, I smile. In a matter of minutes, my world can stop spinning.

I reach my hand out and place my thumb on the scan pad. The door unlocks. As I reach for the handle, an arm slinks around my waist and pulls me backward—hard.

My mouth opens to scream, but it's instantly covered up with a massive hand.

"Shh! Don't scream, baby. It's only me," Hawk whispers hot against my ear.

I'm instantly paralyzed with fear. My eyes dance around hoping someone will see us and help, but he's managed to pull me behind the tall shrubs so we're completely hidden from the street.

As his fingers press into my skin, my mind shouts at me to stomp on his foot and run like hell, or fight to get out of his hold at the very least. But I don't do any of that. Instead, I just stand here, too scared to even breathe. My worse nightmare is coming true and I have no idea how to stop it.

Slowly, he turns me around to face him and moves his hand from my mouth but keeps his grasp firmly on my hips, not giving up an inch of his hold on me. His eyes warn me not to scream. I'm not sure if I could anyway. My vocal cords seem to have shriveled up.

His eyes rake me up and down. An expression of disbelief and awe covers his face when he meets my eyes again.

"God, I've missed you," he says, pulling me into a tight embrace. What little air I had in my lungs is squeezed out in his vise-like hold.

Against his inescapable grasp, I try again to form a sentence. "Hawk, what are you doing here?" I try my hardest to sound casual. I can't let him see that he scares me. He'll use it against me if I do. Staying indifferent is the only card I have to play.

He releases me to tip up my chin to lock eyes with his. "I've come for you. Like I promised." His thick lips form a perfectly wicked smile.

Something inside me snaps.

"Well, I don't want you. Now let me go," I hiss, pushing hard against his grasp.

His smile fades into a hard line and he snickers.

"Yes you do. You just don't know it yet."

I wriggle against him again, growing angry.

"Hawk, let me go or I'll scream!"

He lowers his lips to my ear. My body goes rigid at his touch, so foreign and cold.

"No, you won't." He kisses my forehead and I cringe. "I just want to see my daughter. Then I'll go. I promise."

He releases his grip on me enough so I can see into his eyes. A genuine look of longing is there—and not for me, but for the chance to see his daughter.

"Come on, Jada, you owe me this much. I have the right to see her. Just one visit and I'll go. I just—I need to see her. Please, Jada."

The man standing before me looks so broken and sad. His shoulders have grown slack and bags of sleeplessness droop under his eyes. Is it so wrong for him to at least see his daughter? She may be the only family he'll ever have… It would be cruel to deny him this.

"Fine. But just for a few minutes. Got it?"

Hawk's eyes brighten. For a moment, I catch a glimpse of the boy I new in high school. Maybe all he needed was a second chance. Someone to believe in him, someone who wouldn't abandon him like his own parents and friends had. He lost everything the day he saved me from my father's abusive hand. He's right. I do owe him this visit.

"Thank you, Jada." A tear seems to form in his eye, but he blinks it away before it's allowed to fall.

He links his arm in mine and I lead him upstairs to meet his daughter.

CHAPTER FIVE

Tobias

I'm in the bathroom, madly throwing toiletries into a pillowcase, when I hear the door open downstairs.

Thank God!

I close the cabinet and rush down the stairs. "I've got us almost packed. We can leave anytime now—"

My feet almost fall out from under me while I descend the stairwell as my eyes find Jada's—and Hawk's. His arm is latched on to hers.

"Where are you going this time, Jada?" Hawk probes. She sputters to try and come up with an answer when she's cut off by another voice in the room.

"Daddy!" Janelle screams, jumping off the couch where just moments ago she'd been humming some tune I'd never heard. She runs toward Hawk, who's just as shocked as I am that Janelle just called him "Daddy."

Janelle rushes and attaches herself to his leg. Hawk looks quickly at Jada, then at me. A wicked smile seeps across his face for just a second before he turns his attention back onto Janelle.

"She's beautiful," Hawk whispers, resting his hand on her head of curls.

"Don't you touch her!" I growl, ready to rip off his arms.

"No! It's okay," Jada says, holding up her hand to stop my attack. "I invited him up." She swallows. "It's only fair he meets her." She looks down at Janelle, who raises her hands, wanting to be picked up by Hawk. I have to force my feet not to move as he lifts her and holds my daughter to his chest.

"He just wants to see her," Jada says. "Then he'll go." She glances at Hawk, who's rubbing his nose against Janelle's.

He's not going to just leave after meeting Janelle. No chance in hell.

"My beautiful girls," Hawk coos. "Daddy's home." He nuzzles his face against Janelle again, and I can't help it. I lose it.

Lunging toward him with all my strength, I crash into him, but not before he pushes the girls aside. His shoulder takes the brunt of my blow, but it doesn't knock him over.

"So that's how it's gonna be, is it?" Hawk shouts at me. The muscles in his neck bulge out so I can clearly see the blood coursing through his veins.

Behind me I see Jada pulling Janelle safely into her arms.

"You've seen her. Now get out of my house," I spit back at him.

Hawk has the gall to smile at me. "Or what? You're going to make me? Don't forget, Tobs, *I'm* the stronger one here." He takes a step forward. It's small but intentional. "I don't want to hurt you. Besides, I have every right to be here. She's *my* daughter, not yours."

I try not to let the truth of his words affect me. I know I'll get the shit kicked out of me if this were to come to blows. I don't want Janelle to have to see that. But, then again, maybe getting into a fight will distract Hawk long enough for them to get out of the apartment. It's not much of a plan, but it's the only one I have. This time, I take a step forward.

"Tobias, stop!" Jada shouts, stopping my advance. "Let's not get crazy here." Janelle squirms in her arms, her bottom lip quivering. I hate that she's scared, that I'm the one making her scared.

Hawk seems to relax his posture a bit, but I keep my guard up. I'm not taking any chances.

"Why are you here?" I ask Hawk as calmly as I can.

Hawk gestures toward my family. "I came to see them, of course." He takes a few steps closer so we're practically nose to nose. He towers over me, as he always has, but it's somehow more intimidating now. His once-perfect hair that I'd always been jealous off is still shaved short from prison, adding even more menace to his look. After a mini stare-down of his icy blues, he leans in so only I can hear what he has to say.

"They're mine, and you know it. That's why you're so scared." He draws back. His eyes are cold and unflinching, territorial.

"I want you out of my house, now."

My hand digs into my pocket for my e-port. Enough of these games; I'm calling the cops. Hawk smiles at me. "Looking for something?" He shakes my e-port in his hand. He must have lifted it from me a second ago.

"Give it back."

He reaches out his hand as though to hand it over but then drops it to the ground before he crushes it with the heel of his foot. The cracking of the screen into shards echoes in our tiny apartment.

Beside him, Jada gasps while Janelle cocks her head looking up at Hawk and then down at the shiny bits now on the floor. In that moment, I know this isn't going to end well.

Jada

I watch in disbelief as bits of metal crunch under Hawk's foot. Janelle is clinging onto my hair, pulling it, as though afraid to let it go.

As Hawk turns to smile at her, I catch a glimpse of something tucked in the back of his pants—something sinister lurking there. From this angle it looks like the handle of a very large hunting knife.

This is a game changer. My breath stops. No longer do I believe that he has any plans of leaving here peacefully. *I was a fool to bring him up here!* I trusted him. I felt sorry for him, and all this time, he was just using me to get to my daughter. He won't touch her. Not while there is breath in my body, which means I'll have to get him away from my family. But how? I got us into this mess; it's up to me to get us out, even if it means using myself as human bait.

"Tobias," I say. "I actually think Hawk and I should talk. Privately," I add. Beside me, I feel the burn of Hawk's eyes on me; I can almost sense the smug smile creeping onto his face.

"What? No way, Jada!" Tobias tries to take a step toward me, but Hawk stops him easily with his outstretched hand. Tobias tries to bat his hand away but isn't successful. Things will get ugly if I don't get the two of them away from each other.

"It's okay, Tobias. We need to talk. Alone. I owe him that much." I do my best to telepathically communicate to Tobias that he needs to use this time to get Janelle out of here. "We could go for a walk. Maybe down by the water?" I direct this last sentence to Hawk.

I feel his calloused hand slink inside mine. Goosebumps, and not the good kind, cover my skin.

"I would like that." He smiles at me.

Keeping on my forced smile, I turn my attention back to Janelle and rub her nose with mine.

"Nell, baby, Mama's gonna go for a little walk. I need you to stay here and finish cleaning up breakfast with Papa."

Janelle juts out her bottom lip. "Don't go with Daddy, Mama. Stay with Papa!"

I bite my lip hearing her call Hawk that.

"I can't believe you told her about me," Hawk says, almost in awe.

I look up and see that Tobias is practically crawling out of his skin. His fists are clenched and his eyes are fixed on Hawk. I have to act fast before things get worse.

"Tobias, can you call work and let them know I won't be back in today?" I say, handing him my e-port.

Call the police. Get Janelle somewhere safe, I plead silently. The smallest flicker of recognition shifts on his face. His jaw clenches as he seems to process what I'm asking him to do.

If he knew Hawk had a knife on him, there's no way

in hell he'd let me leave, so I have to get out of here fast before either one of them does something stupid.

"I'll give you ten minutes, but no more," Tobias spits out. "If you're not back by then, I'm calling the police."

"Fine," I say before Hawk can protest. Ten minutes should be more than enough time to get them out of here.

"Nell, honey. Mama will be back in ten minutes. Then we'll play babies, okay?" Janelle just shakes her head but then pulls the fistful of my hair to her lips and kisses my hair, and not me, good-bye.

I put her down and do my best to keep tears at bay. She can't see me crying. She can't know how scared I am.

She returns to Tobias, who scoops her willingly into his arms.

Hawk has re-laced his hand in mine, so I yank him to the door.

I give a final glance at my family. Janelle is hugging Tobias's neck with a small pout on her face while Tobias tries to bottle his rage.

I can only pray they're both long gone before we return.

Tobias

As the door closes behind them, my heart hardens. Jada's "secret" message to me was as clear as day: get out before we return. Too bad I'm not about to let her out of my sight. I don't trust Hawk. He's up to something. Jada was scared. She saw something. There's no way I'm leaving her alone with him.

I press my ear to the door, waiting for them to clear the stairwell. Once they've gone, I scoop Janelle up in my arms.

"Wanna go visit Ms. Skillings?"

"Yeah!" she says. Janelle loves playing with Ms. Skillings, even more than children her own age.

I open the door and walk down the hall and knock. Ms. Skillings is always home. She's an elderly lady that lives just down the hall from us. She's always happy to look over Janelle.

After I get Janelle settled, I'll follow them to the water. Jada must think I'm insane if she expects me to leave her alone with that man. No way in Hell.

Jada

I close the apartment door behind me and feel suddenly cold. Maybe this wasn't the best idea.

"Shall we?" Hawk says, grinning down at me. He loops his arm around my waist.

I nod slowly. I'm stalling. I have no clue what I'm doing right now. "There's this great picnic area we could go to." *A very public area.* This time of day always hosts lots of moms in the park. And police.

Instead of answering me, he just smiles a strange half smile. When we get to the lobby door, he tightens his hand on my hip and leads me through.

"Hawk…" I say, trying to find my backbone. "You're

kind of hurting me." I glance down at his hand that's slinked around me, hoping he'll take the hint and let me walk on my own.

"I know."

He doesn't look at me but focuses dead ahead.

"So let go of me," I hiss. I'm feeling braver knowing he probably won't try something out in the open.

He laughs but doesn't remove his hand.

"Hawk, I'm serious. Get your hands off me!"

Stopping suddenly, he turns his head, cocks it to the side, and glares at me.

"We can either do this my way, or we can go back to your place now and we can talk about my custody rights." His jaw sets in a menacing scowl. I do *not* want him to take me back. We've only been gone a couple minutes. I need to stall for more time. If it means he puts his hand on my hip, then I guess I need to live with it, at least for a few more minutes.

"Fine," I spit. "The park is right across the street."

"I knew you were a smart girl," he whispers, gripping my side with what I know is intentional force. I'll have a bruise there for sure. I clamp my mouth shut, refusing to let him see the pain his grip inflicts. I won't give him the pleasure.

When we get to the crosswalk, I press the button to get to the park, but the second I've pushed it, he pulls me away.

"I don't want to go to the water," he says. "I have a better place in mind."

Annoyed that he's continuing with his little power trip, I follow along with him. At least the direction he's leading me will put more distance between us and the apartment, and right now that's my main objective.

"Okay… so no water. Where are we going instead?"

He squeezes my hand. "You'll see."

A moment later, he's pulling me down the Metro stairs. The Orange Line. *Where in the world is he taking me?*

Tobias

After closing the door to Ms. Skillings's apartment, I too descend down the stairwell that Jada and Hawk just took, flying down the steps two and three at a time. I have ground to make up.

I try not to pay attention to an old tug against my lungs. I just walked too fast, that's all. My asthma is *not* returning. Just because Jada isn't with me doesn't mean it's coming back. I've been fine when she's been gone to work… but then again, she wasn't in danger then.

Outside the apartment, I head toward the water. I know exactly what spot Jada was talking about. It's a great little place right along the riverbank. There's a small children's playground and a sandbox that Janelle could waste the rest of her years playing in. We take her here every weekend, rain or shine.

As soon as I cross the main drag, I should be able to spot them. Of course, I'll have to hide myself behind the line of trees that border the picnic area. If I'm lucky, the wind will work in my favor and I might be able to pick up some of their conversation.

After I cross the pothole-laden tar, however, I don't

easily spot them. I just assumed they would sit at the bench we always use, but right now, it's empty.

Walking closer to the playground, I scan the crowds for Hawk's telltale bleach-blond hair, but all I can make out is the typical Franco-American sea of brunettes.

That's when the panic starts to creep in. *What if they're not here?*

I run now, not caring in the least if I'm spotted or even about the weakening of my breath. I just want to make sure she's here and okay. With my heart starting to thrum in my chest, I look from table to table. Nothing.

Closer to the water, there's still no sign of them. I stop mid-stride when it hits me. *She's not here, Tobias. Can't you feel it? Can't you tell she's nowhere close to you anymore?*

I hate to admit it to myself, but I *can* tell. I've always been able to sense Jada, always able to find her when she was in danger. Each time, my feet have pulled me to her, but now... now I feel nothing, nothing except an ache building inside my lungs. A dangerous ache.

Two thoughts enter my mind at the same time: either he's taken her far away where I can't feel her, or she's...

No. I can't think about that option. I just can't.

All I can do now is return home and wait for them to return. Hawk wouldn't be crazy enough to have me call the cops. When they do come back, however, I'll be prepared.

CHAPTER SIX

Jada

As we descend the stairs into the Metro, the darkness swallows us from view and I feel strangely claustrophobic all of a sudden. Even though we're surrounded by other passengers, the tunnel is somehow more intimate.

I find myself looking up at Hawk as people form around us, talking in rapid-fire succession in their native Canadian French. He seems to have a bit more color than when I saw him last, but perhaps he just looked so pale then because of the lighting. His hair, although still short, has managed to maintain the sun-kissed look he had in high school. *Oh how things have changed since then.* As he stands beside me, I can't help but see the lines etched into the corners of his eyes. Lines not formed by laughing, but from anger and frustration. Lines formed by years in solitude.

"How's Ms. G doing?" Hawk asks. "I stopped hearing from her a while ago. Guess she gave up on me, too."

My mouth opens. *He doesn't know she died.*

"Hawk, she didn't give up on you... She passed away, three months ago."

Hawk whips his head around to me.

"What?"

"It was her heart. She went in her sleep. She wasn't in any pain."

His face contorts and grows red.

"And no one bothered to tell me?!"

The anger in his voice draws the attention of a few people beside us, and instantly he pulls himself together.

"Why didn't Tobias tell me?" He seethes quietly beside me.

Instantly, I feel guilty. I knew they were close. Why didn't I tell him?

"I'm sorry… I guess I thought you'd find out."

"From who, Jada? Ms. G was the only person who even spoke to me while I was in prison." The hurt is evident behind his eyes. He'd been left all alone. He'd been abandoned. I knew what that felt like.

"I'm sorry," I say again.

He straightens his shoulders and cracks his neck. "Whatever. It doesn't matter anymore."

He reaches into his pocket just then and pulls out a small white cloth. He glances at me and smiles. He takes the cloth and rubs it in small circles against his neck. It's not all that hot out so the gesture seems odd. Then again, everything about Hawk is proving to be odd.

As he pockets the cloth, I catch a whiff of cologne. I crinkle my nose involuntarily. I hate that stuff. Why on earth is he putting on cologne, in a subway?

"Where are we going, Hawk? And what do you want from me?" It's the question I've been dying to ask him. The sick, twisted part of me wants to know why he's messing with us. What is his endgame?

"I came to see you," he says with more sincerity than he has any right to have.

"Why? We're not together, Hawk. You know this, right? Janelle may be your biological daughter, but I'm with Tobias. And I always will be."

The words are cruel and perhaps presumptuous on my part, but why else would anyone hunt down a person the way he did? If he thinks I have feelings for him, I need him to know, point blank, that I don't.

"You're with Tobias, but not for long." His statement isn't said with a level of conceit, but with assurance in himself.

"What's that supposed to mean?" I say, glaring up at him.

Hawk turns me to him and forces his arms around me, caging me against his chest. I don't bother to struggle because I'm all too aware of what he's hiding under his jacket.

"It means," he whispers, "that soon you won't be able to take your hands off me, and your boy Tobias will be nothing but a bad taste in your mouth."

I try to pull away from him, but he holds me in place. I want to cry, but I refuse to in front of him. I won't give him the satisfaction.

When the train finally pulls up in front of us, I start to panic. My gut tells me not to get on this train with Hawk. Instinctively, I take a step backward, but he grabs me by the wrists and pulls me close to him.

"We agreed to do this my way, remember?" he growls, not liking the attention we're gathering.

He's right. But more importantly, Tobias needed

more time. I *had* to do everything I could to give them a running start. I'd meet up with them some way when I returned.

If you return, my head shouts.

Ignoring reason, I let Hawk lead me onto the waiting car. Only a handful of other people are in this section of the train. Two teenagers lean against a pole near the back. They're speaking in English about a movie they've just seen. Lots of blood and guts. An elderly woman is talking to a man who appears to be snoozing in one of the seats near the door. Her accent is so thick that I only pick up the word "bacon" from their one-sided conversation.

Hawk brings us over to a cluster of seats covered in red plastic. Although the trains are spotless, a thick layer of stale air seems to stick to your skin, dragging you down.

As the train pulls out of the station, I focus my eyes on the Metro map digitally displayed above the doors, trying to figure out where he's taking us. We're currently on the Montmorency Line. The Orange Line is kind of like a large U that takes a sharp left at one end. The Blue Line is the only other line it connects with. I'm thinking we must be transferring there, since there's not much but residential places past that.

I'm focusing on the map when Hawk suddenly nuzzles his nose into the nape of my neck and I have to restrain myself from smacking him.

"Hawk. Please stop that."

He ignores me and playfully bites the edge of my ear.
"Why should I?"

I push him off me. He is way out of line.

"Because I don't like it!" I bark. "You need to understand that I'm with Tobias, Hawk. Get that through your thick head. I didn't agree to talk with you so you could manhandle me."

He pulls away, but not much. "Why *did* you agree to talk with me, then? And alone, if you didn't still have feelings for me?" His face contorts into a smile; an overwhelming air of cocky arrogance sprawls across his lips.

I swallow down what I want to say to him because as he slinks back into his seat, the knife he's concealing peeks out and I'm reminded of why I need to be cautious with him. I can't make him mad.

Thinking, I try to come up with a plan. By now, Tobias and Janelle should be out of the apartment, so all I have to do is ditch Hawk. A connection to the Blue Line is coming up. If we continue on to Jean-Talon, I should be able to jump off there before the doors close and hop a Blue Line back to the Orange. There is enough foot traffic there to get lost in the crowd at this hour. But I'd need to time it out perfectly. And he'd need to let go of my hand, which is still firmly locked on mine.

How can I get him to let go of my hand?

Four more stops till we reach the Blue Line transfer. Four more stops to come up with a distraction.

The train slows again, and the teenagers get off, leaving the car to just the sleeping old man and his wife who seems to have given up speaking to him and has now lost herself in an e-book. That's when the idea hits me. I know how to get his hands off me.

I look up to the heavens and whisper a silent prayer.

Forgive me, Tobias, for what I'm about to do.

As the train picks up speed, my heartbeat does as well. *Here goes nothing.*

"You're right," I say quietly, squeezing Hawk's hand. He looks at me funny. "About what?"

"You're right about everything. I *have* secretly wanted you all this time and have only settled for Tobias." I swallow down the sickness brewing in my belly and give him my best seductive look, which honestly has never been my strong suit.

Hawk tilts his head to the side, unsure of what to make of me. I have to give him more. Gathering my courage, I try to imagine Tobias. I stare at Hawk's lips, cold and hard, and will them to become the soft and dreamy lips of Tobias. Unable to wait any longer for my imagination to take over, I hitch my leg over his waist and straddle him. His body grows hard under me and it's all I can do not to throw up.

If this is going to work, I need to be aggressive, so I lower my lips to his. The taste of him is so foreign it makes my skin crawl, but I force my tongue into his mouth, thinking only about my escape.

He moans softly as he caresses my tongue with his. I feel his hand release mine and for a half a second, I'm free, but in the next moment, he has both his hands around my waist, caging me on top of him. If I can keep this up a little longer, he won't expect it when I rip away from him and run off the train.

His fingers dig into my flesh, pulling me closer to him. With tears burning in my eyes, I bury my hands in his hair and try to replicate his intensity.

I pull off of his lips and go after his neck instead. I

can't stand the feel of his lips on me a second longer. I bite along the edges of his neck, hoping to come off as sexual instead of aggressive.

As I drag my tongue across his neck, I notice the taste of his skin is strange. Foreign and oddly... attractive?

Suddenly, my head feels weird. Hawk's scent is overwhelming. It seems to consume me—turning me on. I try to remember he repulses me, but my body doesn't seem to agree. Kissing Hawk's neck is almost hypnotic. Seductive, new, exciting.

Jada, stop!

I yank my mouth from his neck, shocked by what I just did.

"I shouldn't have done that," I whisper, panting down at him.

Hawk smiles a crooked grin at me. His hands inch up my spine and my body shakes with anticipation, betraying me.

"No. What you shouldn't have done was stop," he says hot against my neck.

His heady scent envelops me again. My head spins like I'm drunk. I'm not sure what's going on with me. I don't seem to have control of my actions. Unable to stop myself, I give in to his kiss, surrendering to the way his arms feel against my flesh.

My brain doesn't even register when the train stops at Jean-Talon and then goes right past it—along with my escape plan. I am simply too lost inside Hawk's embrace to care.

Tobias

Racing back to the apartment, I feel sick to my stomach. I hate that I'm returning home without Jada. Where did he take her? All I can think is that they'd better be back when I return. If they aren't—

Don't think about that. Just get home.

The trip back to the apartment is a blur. I don't even remember crossing the street. By the time I make it into the building, though, I know I'm in trouble. My lungs hurt. Bad. Cursing, I crawl back up the four flights of stairs to our apartment. The pain has gone from annoying to worrisome. A coughing fit starts on the last landing. It's all I can do to get into the apartment without passing out.

Fortunately, I know exactly where my inhaler is and scramble into the bathroom for its healing mist. Collapsing onto the lip of the tub, I inhale several medicated puffs until my racing heart subsides and my lungs finally expand enough to take some shallow breaths.

As I take in air, I focus on my neon-yellow inhaler. I haven't needed to use this stupid thing in three years. That's when it dawns on me. Something terrible has happened to Jada. I know this because I'm getting sick again.

Although it took me a while to realize she was the cure to my diseased lung, when I did, the rationale was crystal clear. Before I met Jada, I was always one asthma attack away from death, but after I met her, when I had an attack, she would show up and my asthma magically got better. Since we've been together, my symptoms have basically disappeared. Even my doctors can't believe my recovery, but Jada and I knew. It's because we're connected. Twin Flames.

We don't tell many people about out unique connection because not many would believe it. They'd just roll their eyes and chalk it up to us being helpless romantics. But after everything Jada and I have been through, we know we could be nothing else than the other's missing half. Neither one of us ever felt whole until we met each other. We complete each other, and now that she's missing, a part of me is gone too. A vital part, one I need in order to find her: working lungs.

When I try to stand up to check the window, they burn again, only this time they feel like they're about to collapse.

I lean over against my knees, gulping for air that is suddenly hard to catch. My hands dig into my sides. Fire burns inside my lungs. Intuitively I know. Something bad just happened, something that has pulled Jada far away from me.

I need to find her before my lungs give out.

CHAPTER SEVEN

Jada

As my lips curl around Hawk's earlobe I hear a far-off voice asking why I'm still kissing him. I can't come up with an answer. It's as though my body is being forced into these revolting positions. I have no control to stop myself. It makes no sense. All I can seem to focus on is his scent. He just smells so *good*. It's intoxicating: musky, heady, and all sorts of sexy.

I'm so engrossed in his fingers running up the arch of my back I don't notice the snickers coming from passengers who have just boarded.

"We've got an audience," Hawk murmurs in my ear.

"So," I say, licking his neck, which is *so* not like me.

He laughs at me but drags me off his lap. I actually hear myself groan when he forcibly removes me from his body.

I have to hold myself back from going after him for more. I let out a deep breath to try and steady myself.

Jada! What is wrong with you?

My thoughts plead with me to move away from Hawk, but I have no desire to do that. In fact, all I want to do is crawl back on his lap, but the way his hand has latched onto mine tells me he wouldn't allow it even if I tried. Instead, I content myself to just look at his cool ice-blue eyes. I'm hardly able to remember why I ever found them so creepy before. I sink my body against his side, desperate for as much contact as he'll allow. He smirks down at me. Something about his grin tells me he has me right where he wants me, which makes me oddly content—happy even.

The voices protesting against my skull fade into the background when Hawk pulls me closer to him.

"I knew you'd come around," Hawk whispers against my hair. "We're meant to be together, baby. We're meant to be."

Nuzzling up against his side, I smile and close my eyes, buried against his chest. When I'm this close to him, it's surprisingly easy to ignore the screams gurgling in the pit of my stomach

When the Metro comes to the end of the line, Hawk slides his hand in mine, and I take it willingly. His skin is so rough and strong. Such an odd contrast to what I'm used to.

It takes him no effort at all to pull me out of the train. I am his willing slave.

As we make our way to the exit, I lean against him, breathing in his delicious heady scent. Hawk kisses my hair over and over as we climb the stairs to the street.

Montmorency used to be one of the biggest stops on the line years ago, but once the university closed its doors, it became a bit of a ghost town. I can't help but wonder where he's taking us.

As we crest the stairs, Hawk wraps his arm around my waist and holds on tight, almost like he's afraid I'm going to run. I smirk at the idea. I never want to leave his side. Grasping his side tighter, I take a deep breath of the early summer air. Its crisp scent washes over me, filling my senses with memories of the first time Tobias and I moved here...

Tobias...

My head jerks from Hawk's shoulder. His hand presses harder against my waist as though he'd been expecting this reaction.

Outside in the mid-morning air, the reality of what I just did with Hawk on the Metro makes me nauseous.

I just made out with Hawk! In public! Why did I do that? My insides roll. It all comes crashing back. The plan had been to escape from Hawk, not to enjoy his touch. So why *had* I enjoyed it? I'm both disgusted and appalled by what I did with him.

It makes no sense, though! It's not like he could have drugged me or anything. I didn't eat or drink anything while I was with him. But my reaction back there was *not* me.

"Just a bit farther," Hawk whispers hot in my ear. My head spins a little from his proximity. My eyes flutter and I smile at him. *What the hell is happening to me?*

Hawk pulls me tighter to him, almost smothering me as we walk. My head reels with conflicting thoughts. I want to kiss him and punch him all at the same time. I struggle to get a grip on what is happening to me as he drags me toward an old college campus.

An old *abandoned* campus.

Finally, my body takes over and my feet plant to the ground, halting his footsteps.

"Where are you taking me?"

He looks me in the eye. I know he's strong enough to drag me wherever he wants me to go, even in public, so

I don't actually expect him to answer me.

"I'm taking you home." His blue eyes pierce into mine.

"What are you talking about? I have a home. With *Tobias!* And I want to go back there, now!" I swallow back some of the fear that's begun tingling along my skin.

He laughs. "That's not the impression you gave me on the train." Something behind his eyes doesn't seem as shocked as I am about my behavior. Almost like he'd planned this whole thing, but that is impossible.

My cheeks burn with embarrassment. "Look, what happened back there—it was a mistake. I don't know what came over me. I love Tobias—"

He covers my lips with his finger. "Don't say his name again. Do you understand? What you did on the train wasn't the mistake. Your life with *him* was. A mistake I plan on fixing." He releases his hand from my face, but all I can do is gape open-mouthed at his audacity. My head is remarkably clear now.

I'm done with his manipulation. If he wants to risk killing me in public, so be it, but I am *not* about to go anywhere with him.

Although I try my hardest to rip my body out of his hands, he just holds on tighter. His fingers dig deep into my flesh, so firmly that I know they will leave several grape-sized bruises, but I resist the urge to cry out in pain.

"Let go of me, Hawk!" I hiss.

In a flash, he pins my arms to my side and speaks quickly into my ear. "Would you rather I go back and take Janelle instead?" His eyes flick down to his knife.

He knows I've seen it on him.

An unspoken understanding passes between us in the summer wind.

"You wouldn't," I whisper, feeling my body turn to Jell-O.

"Try me." His eyes are cold, wicked. He tugs at my shirt, pulling me forward.

I have no choice. I have to go with him. Gaping up at him, I see his plan etched along the creases in his eyes. He knew just what button to push to get me to submit to his wishes. *Bastard!*

With each step we take, I feel my body start to shut down. It's an oddly familiar feeling. One I used to have when my father was alive. A feeling I never thought I'd have to endure again. I had thought my days of torture were over when my dad died, but now I see they are just beginning. Whatever lies ahead for me on that deserted campus will not end well.

Tears streak down my face at the helplessness of my position. I can't risk running. I *can't* risk him going after my daughter. She is my entire world. I will not allow him to touch her again.

Knowing that my baby is safe with Tobias, my legs find the courage they need to keep moving forward.

Tobias

Almost a half hour has passed and still no sign of Jada. Unless I can get my air back, I'm not going to be able to go out again and look for her. I don't even have enough breath to call the stupid cops!

Before I pick up Janelle from next door, I know I have to get my meds. I'm getting into some dangerous territory here. The inhaler isn't cutting it.

Dragging my feet across the floor, I dig around the cabinet to find my emergency tabs. The bottle shakes as my fingers struggle to remove the cursed cap.

Exhausted, I press one against my tongue. The artificial cherry taste dissolves instantly. I hate taking them because they make me so groggy.

I need to get my compact breather on and get at least a few minutes of that going, but even the idea of climbing the stairs to grab it from my room seems like an impossible task. Maybe if I just lie down on the couch for a second, I'll gather enough strength to make the stairs. I have to be strong. I have to be ready for them when they come back, or at least to search again. I just need to close my eyes for just a second.

I swear I've barely closed my eyes when I hear a light knock on the door. My heart sprints as I lift my body. Before I can answer, Janelle's head pokes in from the front door.

When she sees me, she beams at me and runs to give me a hug, climbing right on top of me. Ms. Skillings follows right after, mumbling her apologies.

"I'm sorry, Mr. Garret. Janelle kept telling me you were home and that you needed help and we needed to check on you. She wouldn't take no for an answer. I didn't think you'd actually be here, though." She gives Janelle a concerned look. "*Are* you okay, Mr. Garret?"

My lungs betray me and a coughing fit ensues instead of the "I'm fine" reply I had planned.

Without my even asking, Janelle runs up the stairs and into my room. I have no idea how she knows I need my nebulizer, but her little hands have the bag and she's dragging it down the stairs. I've never even used it in front of her before, never had the need to. *How did she know I needed this?*

Coughing, I sit up as Janelle plops the bag at my feet. Ms. Skillings rushes to my side and helps Janelle dig the machine out of the bag.

As soon as it's plugged in and the mask encases my nose, I can feel the mist working its way down into my lungs. The cool tingle works almost at once, smothering the fire within.

Not daring to leave me alone, Ms. Skillings sits beside me, reassuring Janelle that I'll be okay. I try to tell them both that I'm fine, but over the hum of the medicine, they can't understand me.

Ms. Skillings swats my hand away when I try to remove the mask and pushes me back onto the couch. She grabs the quilt draped over the couch, *my* quilt, and tucks it under my chin. The effect of my pills is kicking in. My eyelids are getting heavy, despite my desire to stay awake. Without wanting to, I drift off into a deep and medicated sleep.

Jada

I'm able to keep my feet moving forward until we actually get to the campus. As we approach the gate, my pace slows and my muscles become tight with fear.

Weeds and tall grass have overtaken the property from years of neglect, leaving it almost hidden from the occasional cars that pass by.

Mentally, I begin to prepare myself for anything. I've been hit before, so I can take the abuse he can dish out. I'm a pro at shutting down my emotions, even though the thought of enduring it again makes me want to throw up.

Hawk walks to the iron gate that closes off the property to the public. He glances over his shoulder, checking out the non-existent traffic, before he pushes the gate open and pulls me inside.

When he closes the gate, I can see the remains of the chain that he must have cut his way through earlier. That one random detail makes me shiver. This isn't just a lunatic on the loose; this is a man with a well thought out plan.

He pulls me inside. His grasp is so firm that my hand has lost all feeling in my fingertips. We walk in silence for what feels like hours, even though I know it's only been a few minutes. When you're counting down what may be your last moments, time seems to go a little slower. I can't help but think about all the times I didn't say I love you enough to my family. How I'll never see my baby's beautiful face again. How Tobias will never know how sorry I am for agreeing to go with Hawk in the first place. This whole thing is my fault.

All my limbs start to go numb as he drags me up the graveled driveway of what looks like a former frat house. He pulls out a large ring of old-school keys and opens a series of fresh locks on the door. I didn't think they even made scan-free locks anymore.

Although it's dark inside, I can make out a dingy couch that lines the far edge of the room. Stuffing is coming out of one of the arms and a large brown stain marks one of the cushions. Behind the couch, the windows have all been sealed up with what looks like black garbage bags. A small fireplace lies off in the corner. The smell of smoke still lingers from a fire recently burned. Cobwebs line the corners of the walls and between the newel posts lining a banister that leads upstairs.

It looks like two rooms lead away from the living area. Both doors are closed.

Looking into the kitchen, I see a random assortment of nonperishable food that sits undisturbed on top of a table in the kitchen near the back of the house.

Hawk closes the door behind me and I hear three separate locks snap into place.

"Welcome home, baby."

CHAPTER EIGHT

Jada

Welcome home? Is he out of his mind?

"Hawk, you can't keep me here," I say, trying, unsuccessfully to pull out of his grasp again.

"Wanna bet?" he says, wiggling his eyebrows. A lump forms in my throat. *I'm gonna die here*

Hawk

Finally! She's here. She's ours! Seth cackles in my mind.

I can't focus on quieting him right now because Jada is currently trying my patience. She wasn't supposed to resist me this much.

She doesn't respect us yet. You need to show her you're in charge. Then she won't resist us.

I hate to think he may have a point.

Showing her who's in charge, I drag her by her wrist

across the room.

"Sit down," I order.

Her face contorts and she spits at me.

I don't need Seth for this. She's not going to get away with that. Before she can even blink, I bring my knee up and sink it into her gut, effectively making her double over with pain and collapse onto the couch.

That's more like it!

Charged, I bend down and grasp her hair, holding her still. "When I tell you to do something, you do it. Got it?"

The way she shrinks back from me is affirming.

You need to teach her how we expect her to behave.

I nod in agreement. She'll learn. As she gasps for breath, I head into the kitchen. I'm glad I thought to pick up those ties now.

I told you you'd need them, Seth whispers.

Grabbing the package from out of the bag on the counter, I turn back to Jada.

"These should hold you still until I get you under control." I wiggle the bag of plastic zip ties in front of her. The fear in her eyes is electrifying.

"Hawk," she whispers. "What are you doing?"

I slowly pull out a handful of ties, oddly enjoying that I'm taunting her. She tries to escape from the couch, but I climb on top of her, straddling her petite frame. She's not going anywhere. She bucks her hips hard against me, trying to push me off, but all she's doing is turning me on.

"Shh, baby. Relax. We'll have time for that soon enough, but for now, I need you to stay put."

With ease, I reach down and grab her arm. Jada

continues to struggle against me, even trying to bite me, but her attempts are futile.

She's no match for us.

In a mater of seconds I've laced the tie around her right hand. I slide a second one on her left hand, then lock the two together with a third.

Holding on to her bound writs like you would a dog on a leash, I drag her off the couch. She kicks and flails around like a wild animal. It's amusing to watch.

"Calm down, baby. Save some of that energy for later." With a swift motion, I scoop her off her feet and toss her over my shoulder. Her legs kick wildly until I hook my right arm over them, holding her still. I carry her into the room I've prepped for her. I know it's not much, but I didn't have a lot of time once I got out. I managed to drag this worn mattress from one of the rooms upstairs. The stuffing is coming out on one of the corners, but I threw a sheet I found in one of the closets on it. It's the only thing in the room, except for the radiator that she'll be attached to. *Can't have her trying to escape, now can we?*

I hadn't wanted to tie her, but now I'm glad Seth suggested it. She's far more resistant than I thought she'd be.

Give her time. She'll learn who her master is.

Jada starts screaming when I throw her onto the bed. She probably thinks I'm gonna rape her. I'm not a monster. I'll wait for her to come after me. Until then, she'll have to be trained.

Grabbing another tie from my back pocket, I fasten her to the radiator. Her screams become more frantic.

"Scream all you want doll face. No one will hear you

out here." I push myself off the bed and wipe the sweat from my forehead.

"You're wilder than I remember." I smile down at her in the darkness. "It's gonna be so much fun breaking you," Seth's voice says in place of my own.

I scowl at myself for letting Seth take control. I'm in charge. Not him.

"I'll be back. Don't go anywhere, okay?" I can't help but laugh at my own joke.

Jada

His footsteps take him back out into the living room, and I fight against the tears that want to come. With my heart thundering inside my chest, I struggle against the plastic holding me prisoner, but there is no hope of escape. I know the attempt is futile, but my body still battles for release.

Soon, my voice grows hoarse and my muscles give out from sheer exhaustion. Unable to fight any longer, I let my arms fall limp.

I look around my makeshift prison and try to find a way out. The one window in the room has been covered with that same black plastic material that was in the living room. It manages to not only block out most of the light, but it's also clearly limiting the supply of fresh air inside. I can practically taste the dust that's sure to be coating my lungs. Tobias would not do well here.

Tobias. I begin to quietly sob thinking about him. He must be out of his mind with worry. Hot tears roll down my face as I try to hold on to what may be my last memories of my family.

I do my best to stop the tears when I hear Hawk coming back. I hate that I can't even wipe them from my cheeks. He'll see my tear-streaked face and probably be pleased that he caused my suffering.

When he enters the room, I see that he has a large bowl and a roll of paper towels.

"Your restroom, my lady," he says, placing the bowl beside the bed.

I curse at him again and try kicking the bowl away with my legs. Faster than I can even blink, his hands have caged my legs against the bed. He's so strong that I can't make them budge from beneath his grasp.

"I don't want to hurt you, Jada, so don't make me."

"If you don't want me hurt, then let me go!"

He smiles. "I'll let you go once you let *him* go. Until you realize Tobias is the one poisoning your mind, not me, you'll be restrained. But don't worry. I'll help you forget him soon enough." He traces his finger down my scar, and I'm helpless to move away from him. "Don't forget, it was *me* who saved your life that night because Tobias was too much of a pansy to do it himself. *I'm* the one who sat in a cell for three years so that dick of a father couldn't hurt you anymore." I try to pull my face away, but he grabs my chin and locks it in place. "*I* saved you then, and I'll save you from Tobias's head games now. You and I are meant to be, Jada. And deep down, you know that too."

He throws my legs out of his grasp and marches out of the room again, slamming the door behind him, leaving me alone.

After I've cried myself out, I lay in the darkness, chilled and spent. Time passes and Hawk doesn't return. I can still hear him in the house, clomping from one room to the next—my heart flip-flops each time I think he's coming back, but he doesn't. He just leaves me here, tied up like an animal, scared out of my mind.

My eyes droop with exhaustion after a while and my arms ache from being held over my head for so long. The tingling in my hands left some time ago and now they just feel cold.

I'm just about to drift off into sleep when the bedroom door opens.

A beam of light hits me square in the eye, causing me to squint and casting an odd halo-like effect around Hawk's body. He walks into the room, carrying a small bag. My heart begins to race wondering what he might have inside.

"I thought you might be hungry. I got you a turkey and Swiss." He stands hovering above me as though waiting for me to take it from him.

"I'm not hungry," I spit out, hoping my stomach doesn't give me away.

He crouches down low so I can see his eyes drill into mine. "You're a horrible liar." He drops the bag to the floor and reaches into his back pocket and produces the knife.

I coil back in fear.

"Relax. I'm just cutting you free so you can eat."

He stands up, digs into his back pocket again, and grabs another tie, holding it between his teeth. With the knife, he slices through the tie connecting my hands to the radiator. My arms fall limp at my sides. I still have a tie holding my wrists together, but at least now my hands are in my lap instead of over my head. The blood rushes back into my fingers so fast that it feels like they are on fire. Before I can try to rub the feeling back into them, Hawk has secured the tie that was in his teeth to himself and then to my remaining tie, effectively chaining me to him.

"There," he says, plopping down onto the mattress with me. "Lunchtime."

With his unbound right hand, he grabs the bag and pulls out the sandwich. My stomach lurches at the thought of eating, but something about the way he looks at me when he unwraps the sandwich tells me I'll be eating this thing one way or the other.

I take the offered first bite and swallow it down. It sinks into my stomach like a rock. How many more meals will I have to eat strapped next to him?

Hawk

Once she's asleep, I realize the hard part is over. I got her here. She's safe now. It was easy. Too easy.

You couldn't have done it without me, Seth's voice whispers.

"Like hell I couldn't," I toss back.

Pacing, I walk the floor of the frat house, unable to sleep yet. Jada practically passed out at eleven. Poor thing is worn out. I'll make it up to her. When we get out of here, I'll make sure she never has to lift a finger.

We should leave now! The child will only slow us

down.

"Be quiet!" I say to the darkness. I'm not leaving without my kid; having her here too is the only way this plan is going down. I will have the family I was denied. I'll be an amazing father. I'll show Janelle everything there is to know about hunting. And I'll love her. I show her what real love is. I'll show them both.

Before I can go get her, though, I need to unload the pills I have and get some cash. Then we can get out of here.

Seth does have a point, as much as I hate to admit it. We could just leave now and hide out in the woods and live off the land, but I'm being smart about this. I want a safety net first. I'll need to get some hunting gear too so I can keep us fed.

See, Seth doesn't understand. There's a method to my madness. Not that I'm mad, 'cause I'm not.

Stop wasting time. Get ready for tomorrow.

"That's the best idea you've had all day."

Walking into the kitchen, I light a small candle so I can see what the hell I'm doing. In the dim light, I slip out a small handful of my pills. Grabbing two spoons, I place the pills between them and crush them into a fine powder, just like the druggies do, before I boil it down in the spoon by holding it over the flame. But I'm not gonna be injecting this into my veins. Oh no.

Reaching into my duffle bag, I pull out the one purchase, aside from the knife, that I made before I crossed the border: a bottle of Ralph Lauren Polo. Ricardo's favorite cologne. It was all I had around to experiment on while in prison. One of the other inmates taught me this trick. Confessed that's how he got all his women to obey him.

Twisting off the cover, I pour the liquefied meds inside the cologne and replace the cap. A few quick shakes and tomorrow's plan is ready.

CHAPTER NINE

Tobias

I feel like I'm swimming. Well, not so much swimming as drowning. All around me it's cool and peaceful, but an odd heaviness is pulling inside my chest, pulling me down, away from the light. Away from her.

Frail hands grasp my shoulders, pushing me further into the deep.

"Mr. Garret?" a voice calls out.

I rip myself from a dead sleep to find Ms. Skillings bent over me, shaking me awake.

"I'm sorry to wake you, Mr. Garret, but I really need to check on Fluffy."

"Fluffy?" I say. My voice is muffled and I can't figure out why.

"My cat, Mr. Garrett. She's not used to me being gone so long."

I pry my lids open, suddenly remembering where I am. I rip the medicated mask off my face.

"What time is it?" I shout, my heart thundering. *How much time have I lost?*

Ms. Skillings smiles gently. "It's morning, darling. I stayed here with Janelle last night. I used what I think is your spare bedroom." She gestures past the living room to Ma's old room. A room we haven't used since she passed. "I hope you don't mind," she says, seeing my face contort. "You just looked so tired. I didn't have the heart to wake you."

What?

I bolt upright, a cold sweat forming on my skin. I only have one thought in my mind at the moment.

"Did Jada come back?"

"Jada? Well, no, Mr. Garret. Was she supposed to return?" Worry causes her skin, already lined with age, to crease even more.

Beside her on the floor, Janelle has lifted her head to catch my answer. The poor kid still doesn't know why her mom isn't home yet.

"Um, no. She should be back soon though," I say, more toward Janelle than Ms. Skillings. Janelle juts out her lower lip and I can tell she wants her mama right now.

Ms. Skillings comes over to me and rubs my shoulder, nodding some unspoken gesture of understanding. She probably thinks Jada and I had a fight. How much do I wish it were only that?

"I could go and come right back, if you need me to," she offers.

"No. It's fine. Thank you. Thank you for staying with Janelle. I'm sorry to have put you out."

The courtesies I utter come without any forethought. Jada still hasn't come back! I have to call the police.

Ms. Skillings looks from me to Janelle and frowns, clearly not wanting to leave us. With a sigh, she pulls her light-pink cardigan closed before she says her good-byes to Janelle. Her slight hunched back makes her waddle like a penguin when she walks toward the door.

The moment she steps inside her apartment, I turn to Janelle.

"Nell, peanut, Papa just needs to make a quick call, okay?"

She nods at me and continues watching her show.

As fast as I can, I run upstairs and into our bedroom and press 9-1-1.

"9-1-1, what's your emergency?"

My throat tightens, but I force out the words. "I need to report a missing person."

"How old is the person, sir?"

"She's twenty-one. Look, I think she's been kidnapped—"

"When did she go missing?" The operator's voice is measured, rehearsed. She's reading from a script of scenarios. It's maddening, but I play along so they'll track her down.

Letting out a great exhalation, I tell her she's been missing since nine o'clock yesterday morning.

"I'm sorry, sir. Until she's been missing for a full forty-eight hours, there is nothing we can do."

"What?" I scream. "I'm telling you my girlfriend has been kidnapped and you tell me there's nothing you can do?"

"I'm sorry, sir. Have you tried calling her e-port?"

I grit my teeth trying to be calm. "She doesn't have it on her. I'm telling you, she was kidnapped by a convicted felon. He was with her in my house yesterday morning. They went for a walk and they never came back!"

Even as I say it, I realize how the operator is going to interpret what I've just said. She doesn't believe Jada was kidnapped; she just thinks I've been dumped.

"Argh!" I hang up on the operator before she hangs up on me.

Just then, the intercom goes off downstairs.

Please be Jada!

Flying down the stairs, I tap the screen by the door with my finger, springing it to life. As soon as the image appears, my heart falls. It's not Jada. It's Kari. But why? I press the talk button.

"Kari? What are you doing here?"

She looks up at the camera overhead. Her face looks like she hasn't slept in days. I know the feeling. She doesn't look at all like the middle-aged women we visited at Ma's funeral. She looks at least ten years older.

"Can I come up?" Her voice is tired and clearly laced with worry.

"Of course." I buzz her in. "We're on the fourth floor. Elevator's out. Number 415."

Pacing along the floor, I weigh my options. Janelle comes over and raises her arms, wanting a good cuddle. Scooping her into my arms, I press her close to me, suppressing the cough that's trying to escape my lips. Slowly, Janelle rubs her hand across my chest, the same way she does with Jada's scar.

"Does it hurt, Papa?"

I try not to cry at her question. "No, baby girl. You helped me get my medicine." I kissed her head and she smiles. "Nell, baby, how did you know I needed to have my mask on?"

She just shrugs her tiny shoulders and points to her head.

"I saw in here what would make you feel better."

Confused, I lower her off my hip to the floor and bend down beside her to look her in the eye.

"You saw my breathing machine? In your head?" I can't believe I'm actually asking this of my daughter.

"Uh-huh." She rubs at her nose. "I see all sorts of things up here."

Just then there is a knock at the door, and I almost jump out of my skin. Janelle claps her hands and runs to the door, but I hold her back. Cautiously, I open the door just a crack to make sure it really is Kari.

Her windswept, newly grayed hair confirms her identity, so I open the door all the way.

Kari rushes into the apartment, out of breath from the stupid stairs. I notice right away that she has dark circles under her eyes, the kind you get from days of worry. I know those circles well.

"Did you get my message? Is everyone okay? Did he show up here?" Kari's eyes flick down to Janelle, who smiles up at her.

"Oh, baby girl!" Kari beams. "Peanut! How much you've grown!"

Janelle hugs onto the edge of my pant leg, not hiding, but more trying to figure out where she's seen Kari before.

"This was Grammie's friend, Miss Kari," I tell her, rubbing the top of her curls.

Janelle nods as though in recognition, then says, "She misses you."

"Who?" Kari and I say at the same time.

Janelle giggles. "Grammy. She misses Ms. Kari."

Tears begin to well up in Kari's eyes. "I miss her too, pumpkin."

Knowing I need to have an adult conversation without little ears picking up what we're saying, I take out Janelle's e-sketch pad and set her on the couch to draw. It's her most favorite thing to do and will easily keep her occupied for several minutes while we talk.

After she's set up, Kari and I walk to the kitchen where I put on water to make us some tea.

"Where's Jada?" Kari asks as soon as she's seated.

This time, the tears well up in my eyes. I don't even know how to tell her what happened without completely breaking down in front of my daughter.

"He took her," I whisper. It's all I can get out before I know I'll lose my shit. Even with that, though, I collapse into Kari's arms and sob uncontrollably as I recount the hell we've been through since Hawk darkened our doorstep.

I have lost all ability to remain rational or calm about this anymore. She's been gone far too long for me to think everything is going to turn out okay. The worse case scenarios won't stop playing through my mind.

"I don't know where she is." I moan softly into Kari's shoulder.

"I do."

Janelle's voice resonates even across the room. Instantly, I pull myself together and wipe at my tear-soaked cheeks.

"You do what, baby girl?" Kari asks for me.

"I know where Mommy is."

Kari looks at me; her eyebrows rise in confusion.

Crossing over to where Janelle is drawing, I sink onto the couch beside her. The red pleather nearly swallows me up. I twirl a lock of her hair around my finger, trying to validate her opinion.

"Oh yeah?" I say, putting on my best "interested" voice. It cracks a bit, but I continue. "Where is your mommy?"

She bunches up her porcelain face and closes her eyes. "It's dark there," she begins. I know she's just making the story up as she goes, but the words send chills up my spine anyway. "She misses us, Papa." Janelle looks up at me with the saddest eyes I've ever seen on her. I start to tear up, knowing how true her statement is, but before the tears can fall, Janelle continues. "Don't cry, Papa. Daddy is with her. He's taking care of her."

She gives me a kiss on the cheek and scrambles out of my grasp and goes back to her tablet.

Kari and I look at each other, dumbstruck.

"Janelle, pumpkin, how do you know its dark where your mama is?" Kari asks carefully, taking a step into the living room.

My skin starts to tingle in anticipation of her answer. After all, she *did* hit the nail on the head about Hawk showing up yesterday and about her grandmother passing away... Maybe she has some sort of a gift?

Janelle continues coloring a picture of what I think is a cat. "I can see it." She taps the tablet pen against her lip, like she does when she's concentrating. "She wants us to come get her, Papa. Can we?"

The tears fall this time. "Baby girl… if I knew where she was, I'd bring her home to you right this second."

Janelle's eyes light up with the possibility.

"I can draw it!" she squeals, tapping her screen for a blank page.

Despite all logic, I find myself holding my breath to find out what she comes up with.

Jada

I survived the night. I'm not sure how, but I'm still here. Still stuck in this hell that I can't wake up from.

Although the room is still dark, I can tell the sun is about to rise. A pale sheen of gray manages to worm its way around the covered-up blinds—tiny rays of hope.

I shiver against the cold morning air. The thin blanket draped over me does little to provide my soul any real warmth. Of course, the chill might be coming from what's on the other side of the bed, too. Although he radiates heat in his sleep, I refuse to get closer to him than our bound wrists force me to be.

After he attached himself to me so I could eat yesterday, he decided he liked being connected to me. He told me he liked the feel of my skin against his. I wanted to tell him how repulsed I was each time we touched, but I've learned that the look in his eyes can turn murderous in a flash. If I am going to survive this —*if I want to see my family again*—I need to bite my tongue and do what he says.

Even though I'm awake and my body is begging me to stretch, I remain frozen. I don't want to risk waking up Hawk before I have to. I even ignore wiping away the crusty residue on my face from all the dried-up tears. My bladder is full again, but again, I ignore it.

I'll experience the humiliation of having to ask to go to the bathroom soon enough. Yesterday he tied me to the radiator and watched me pee in a bowl on the floor. The arrogant look in his eyes confirmed that he got off on my dependence on him for even the most basic of human needs. It was a look that told me the worst of this was yet to come.

Beside me he stirs, seemingly awakened by my traitorous thoughts. Quickly, I force my lids shut and pray he'll just go back to sleep.

Instead, he notices the gap between us, grunts, then curls up against me. Pretending I'm still asleep, I let him wrap his arm around me and hold back the urge to kick away from him.

Somehow against the rhythm of his heavy breathing, I slip back into sleep. I dream of Janelle. My baby. My angel. I know she isn't real. But the feeling of my daughter's hands wrapped around my neck is so powerful that I want to stay asleep forever.

I miss you, she whispers in my hair. *I miss you more,* I murmur back to her. Just like that, her curls shrink away. Her soft angelic face shifts into Hawk's deadly glare.

It's my screaming that wakes us both.

"Damn, baby, you could wake the dead with a scream like that," Hawk says, rubbing his eyes with his free hand.

Fresh tears start running down my face despite my desire not to cry in front of him. Hawk curls against me and starts to wipe them away, making me cringe.

"What's wrong?" he asks, stroking my hair.

"I miss my family," I whimper. "Please, my daughter needs me. Please, just let me go."

"I'm your family now," he says, steel in his eyes. "But don't worry. So is Janelle. She'll be with us soon enough."

He kicks off his covers, oblivious to what he's just said.

"No!" I shout, propping myself on my elbows. "Don't you dare touch my daughter!" Struggling, I try to hit him with my free hand. Over and over again, my balled-up fist makes contact with his bare chest. I only get a few shots in before he rolls on top of me and pins my arms over my head.

Panting and breathless, he growls over me.

"She's *my* daughter too."

Sobbing, I struggle under him, baring my teeth even, trying to make contact with his flesh.

"Enough!" he shouts. He lifts his hand like he's going to strike me. His nostrils flare in rage, a rage I've seen enough times to know what happens next. I close my eyes against the waiting blow.

"I think it's time you're forced to obey," he says eventually. I tentatively open my eyes.

Without hesitation, he grabs my wrists and drags me up to standing. He fishes around in his back pocket and produces a fresh tie to secure me to the radiator.

"Freshen yourself up. I'll be right back."

I cower in the bed. My legs curl up as close to my body as I can get them.

"What are you talking about?" my shaking voice pleads.

He stops. The muscles in his back relax. Turning around, he leans his huge body in the doorjamb. "The first step was getting you here. The next step is making sure you never want to leave." An evil grin slinks onto his lips. "Since you seem to still be brainwashed by Tobias, I guess I'm gonna have to speed up the process." He turns again and walks out of the room.

"What are you talking about?" I screech after him.

"You'll see," his bone-chilling laugh fills my eardrums.

My body starts to shake, and not from the cold this time.

CHAPTER TEN

Tobias

"Tobias, you can't be serious?" Kari asks me for the hundredth time as I make Janelle some scrambled eggs with cheese. I've decided that once she comes up with her drawing, I'm going to let her take me to where she thinks her mom is. I know it's crazy, but it's the only lead I have.

"I'm dead serious." I plate Janelle's breakfast and put a few slices of melon on the side. Jada loves melon... She ate it every morning. My eyes water at the memory.

As Janelle eats her breakfast, her tablet still at her side, I take Kari's elbow and lead her into the living room.

Keeping my voice low, I motion for her to sit. After a moment, she sinks into the wing-back that we saved from my mother's place before the estate sale. It has a rip on the armrest so it held no value. The auctioneer said I could keep it. All I have left of my mother are the things he deemed worthless. Fortunately for me, the items of her unsellable estate held vaults full of memories no bidder could match.

"I know it's hard to believe any of this, but yesterday, before Hawk even showed up, Janelle told me he would be coming."

Kari crosses her arms over her wrinkled floral shirt, not believing a word.

"She said she saw in her head that her 'daddy' would be coming to visit. I didn't believe it either, because who would?" Kari raises her eyebrows and tries to speak, but I hold up my hand. "But look what happened? Jada's gone, Kari. He took her, and I have no idea where. If there is even a *remote* chance that Janelle can see where her mother is, then I'm going to take it."

Kari's eyes flick over to Janelle, who is happily munching her fruit. Her little legs dangle over the bar-stool as she chews. She tucks a curl behind her ear. The gesture reminds me so much of Jada that it makes my heart ache.

"I have to find her, Kari," I say. "I have to."

Kari gives me a sad smile. "I know you do." She pats my shoulder. "And we have to talk."

Kari crosses her legs nervously in the chair beside me. Her dark, graying hair has been pulled off her pale face and into a messy bun. Several hairs frame her soft jaw line. Her eyes wrinkle with worry. Something is on her mind.

"What's the matter?" I ask.

She shifts in her chair. Her long fingers lace in and out of each other.

"I think I might be the reason Hawk found out where you were in the first place," she whispers.

I swallow and take a deep breath. I had kind of assumed that but didn't want to admit it.

"What makes you think that?"

Her hands move to her face as though wiping away

the shame of her actions. She stands up and walks over to the window. The way she holds her body reminds me that she's aged. Since I saw her last at the funeral, she seems to have more slump in her shoulders. Deeper wrinkles have made their home along her forehead. Her once-graceful body now seems more like a burden to her than it once was.

"I know I shouldn't have, but I kept the letters your mother wrote to me before she passed." She lets out a great breath of air as though this statement had been weighing her down for years.

"What letters?"

She sighs softly before she meets my gaze.

"We wrote each other letters. Every week. The paper kind." She chuckles quietly. "You know your mother. She'd never resort to digital anything, let alone for something as intimate as a letter."

A large lump forms in my throat at the mention of my mother. Ma was a stubborn one. She never even got an e-port, never wanted one.

Kari yanks at the clip holding up her hair and lets it fall down to her shoulders. She rubs at the base of her head, as though trying to relieve the pressure of her secret.

"I never saw her with any letters..." I say, confused by what this has to do with anything.

Kari smiles. "That doesn't surprise me. She knew how paranoid you were. She hid the letters from you because she knew you'd probably flip your lid if you knew she was writing to me."

I cock my head, not understanding.

"Why would I be upset that you were writing to my

mother? You guys were friends. There's nothing wrong with that."

"We were writing paper letters, Tobias."

"So."

Kari gives me a sad smile. "Paper letters require a return address."

I close my eyes in ignorance. *Of course.*

"He found the letters?"

She lets out a huge breath but nods.

"I know I should have tossed them, but I just couldn't. They were a part of who she was." She sniffs. "Driving by her empty house during those months after her death were the hardest. We used to have tea every morning. Did you know that?"

A fat tear trickles down her face.

"No, I didn't."

Turning from the window, she slowly sits back down in the chair. Her confession is over.

"I'm not upset that you kept them. She would have wanted it that way," I say, wiping the wetness from my own eyes.

"Well, you should be upset with me," she whispers. "If I hadn't been feeling lonely that morning and reading one of her letters when Hawk burst through my door, then you would still have Jada!"

A long silence fills the air while she cries softly into her hands. I know she blames herself, but after what I saw of Hawk yesterday, I know he would have found us eventually, one way or another.

"It was only a matter of time." I try. "He would have found us. Don't blame yourself."

She turns back to me and sits beside me on the couch,

casting a quick glance at Janelle.

"He didn't lift a finger to me, Tobias. He just walked into my house, demanded where Jada was. Then when I didn't answer, he saw the letters sprawled out on my table, took a stack, and left. I called Jada right after he left, but while I was leaving Jada a message, he came back. He took one look at me and marched over to where I was standing and ripped the e-port out of my hands and threw it across the room, breaking it." She shivers at the memory. "He didn't hurt me, Tobias, but I could feel it in my bones that he could have if he wanted to."

My eyes grow hard. Yes. I know exactly what she means, which is why I need to find Jada.

"Did he leave after that?" I ask.

She nods. "After taking my car, bastard. That's why it took me so long to get here. I had to get a new e-port *and* ride the damn train to get to you."

My heart sinks. She doesn't have her car. I'd been relying on her using that to get Janelle out of here.

"All done," Janelle says, hopping off the stool. She wipes her mouth on her sleeve. A bit of egg clings to her flower-print T-shirt. "Can I draw where Mommy is now?"

Kari looks at me, worry creasing her brow further.

"Yes, baby girl. You can draw Mommy now."

CHAPTER ELEVEN

Jada

I listen in petrified silence as Hawk rummages around in the next room. I can't tell what he's doing, but it's clear that he's hurrying. He curses, kicks something across the floor, and then his footfalls head my way.

When he comes back in, he's holding a flannel shirt in his hand. A wicked grin is planted on his lips. He tucks the shirt in his back pocket, then in a flash, releases me from the radiator and flings me over his shoulder.

Kicking and screaming, I try to wiggle out of his grasp. When he carries me out of the room, I still my body, trying to get a better sense of the room and where my hopes of escape might lie.

Little had been changed since he brought me through yesterday. The only thing I notice that's different is the end table next to the couch.

It's covered almost entirely with pills now. Like hundreds of them. Suddenly, Hawk's plan seems all too clear. I am to be drugged.

He tosses me onto the couch where I shrink away from the bottles. His eyes follow my horror struck gaze and he laughs at me.

"What? Scared of a few pills?"

I nod quickly, not daring to speak.

He brushes my hair behind my ears, exposing my scar. After a second, he frowns and pulls the strands back where they were.

Bastard.

"Where did you get those drugs?"

He snorts a little. "From the doctor. They're mine."

I gasp. "All of them?" There was no way one person could take all that medication. "Are you sick?"

He looks over his shoulder to glare at me, as though I've slapped him. "My docs seem to think so." His tone is sharp, almost annoyed. "I'm not crazy, but I played along and let them give me the pills. For two and a half years they gave me these suckers twice a day. Or at least they *thought* they did. I became a pro at faking it." He smiled. "Those pills they tried to get me to use so I could be their controlled puppet backfired. I never took them. Flushed them all. And when they discharged me? They sent me home with a month's supply. A supply I don't need, obviously."

I shake my head slowly, trying to absorb it all.

"How else do you think I'm funding all this? These babies fetch a great price on the street. We won't be here forever. Just until I can get those pills sold. Then it will be better. You'll see."

"Hawk." I try. "Tobias will be looking for me. He'll send out the police. Just please let me go and I won't tell the cops anything."

He sinks down on the couch beside me and grabs both my wrists.

"I'm not worried about the cops *or* Tobias. We'll be long gone before anyone can find us."

From the determination in his voice, it's clear that this frat house is not our final destination. He's going to be moving us. I would assume out of the country as soon as he sells his drugs. My only hope is Tobias or the police will find me soon. If Hawk takes me out of Canada, I know all hope would be lost. We would vanish, just like he wanted.

I try a last ditch effort.

"Please, Hawk. My baby needs me. Please just let me go." I hate the tears that trickle down my face.

"I know she needs you." He shifts his weight and pulls out the shirt he'd tucked in earlier. "Which is why I need you in my full control. If we're going to get her, I need you on my team."

My mouth opens in fear at the insinuation laced in his words.

He starts to bring the shirt to my face. Panicking, I try to turn my head away, thinking he's about to gag me with it, but he grabs the back of my head with his other hand and forces my face into the folds of the fabric.

"Smell it," he orders while holding the nape of my neck in a vise grip.

I can't help but think it's laced with chloroform, so I do my best to hold my breath, but the struggle for air wins out and all too soon I'm forced to take a great intake of the muffled air. I brace myself for the inevitable blackout, but it doesn't come. Instead, I smell that same musky scent I remember Hawk wearing on the train. Warm and delicious.

Warning bells start going off in my head. I try to

piece it together, but suddenly Hawk is looking down at me with his big blue eyes and I can't help but grin at him like a big dope. He's so beautiful.

Hawk's chiseled jaw sets itself into a perfect smile as he removes the shirt from my mouth and ties it loosely around my neck.

"Hey, baby," he breathes against my cheek.

"Hey."

I close my eyes against his hot breath. My head spins a bit, but there is also something else there—need.

My hands itch to run through his hair, but I notice they are bound. I don't remember them being tied up. *Hmm. Kinky.*

"You smell so good," I coo, my voice not sounding at all like my own. My hands strain to touch Hawk. I start with his chest first, amazingly firm against the soft cotton tee he's wearing. I lick my lips, wanting nothing more than to just rip it off of him.

I loop my caged hands around his neck, my fingers drifting up to the back of his shaggy blond hair, and try to pull him down to my lips, but he stops me. He grabs me over his shoulder and lifts me off the couch. I lick his ear as he carries me and he slaps my ass in response, which only drives me wild with desire.

He flops me onto the bed where I try to rip off that T-shirt, but he stops my hands. He reaches behind him and produces another tie and secures me to the radiator. *Fun.* A playful grin spreads across my face.

"I wish I could play with you more, babe, but I have to go unload some of my stash so I can get us out of this dump. I just needed to make sure this stuff worked." He bends over the bed and gives me the shortest of kisses.

So short it's almost cruel. He removes the shirt around my neck and tosses it on the ground where it lands in a dark corner. Almost instantly, my head begins to clear.

My nose stings and my stomach clenches.

"What—what happened?" I cough.

Hawk starts laughing. "Just what was supposed to, Jada. I don't have time to wait around for you to get Tobias out of your head. For this to work, we all need to leave tomorrow at the latest. So until you come around —and you *will* come around—I will just have to use my special brew.

The confusion must be clear on my face—either that or he's been dying to let me in on his little secret— because he comes back to the bed and squats down in front of me.

"See, I made some real nice friends in prison. They knew how to get and *keep* their women. They gave me a quick chemistry lesson on how to do it right so they didn't even know anything was up." He gives me a wicked smile. "Seeing you kiss me the way this will make you,"—he gestures to the shirt—"it's gonna break Tobias's little heart. That's how we'll end this peacefully. You'll tell him it's over with him, that you secretly loved me all along, and we'll take *our* daughter and leave. It's easy really."

My body starts to tremble at the ease with which he rattles off his plan to steal my family away from the man I love.

"Don't worry, baby, I'll be back soon and we'll have some alone time. I promise." He walks back over to me and tries to touch my face, but I turn away from his attempt. My wrists strain against the ties as I try to pull myself as far away from him as they will allow.

"God, I'm gonna enjoy breaking you in." He lets out a soft chuckle. "Be a good girl, now. I'm off to make us some money."

With that, he walks out the door and out of the frat house, leaving me alone with an onslaught of fresh tears.

Tobias

Kari and I walk into the living room to sit next to Janelle as she prepares to draw on her e-pad.

"Okay, baby girl. Where do you think Mommy is?"

Janelle scrunches up her face for a bit, thinking. After a moment, she starts to draw a few lines that don't look like much of anything: two orange parallel lines. Nothing more.

Janelle looks up at us with her pale-blue eyes and points to her drawing.

"Um, what is that, honey?" I ask, trying not to hurt her feelings.

"It's a train!" she says as though it's the most obvious thing in the world. "Can we go too, Papa?"

My heart starts to race. "A train?"

She smiles and nods. "An orange one."

Beside me Kari sighs, thinking this is pointless, but I know exactly what Janelle is getting at.

The Metro. She's talking about the Metro. They're still in Montreal!

Digging out my e-port, I quickly pull up a map of the

Metro. "Can you show me where?" I know it's a long shot, but I can't help but think she might just know where her mother is.

Janelle takes the e-port onto her lap, looking at all the spots on the line. She scratches her nose at one point and I realize, like an idiot, that she can't read yet.

Just as I'm about to start listing off the stops, she puts her finger on the screen: Montmorency.

"You think she went to the Montmorency stop?" I ask, looking up at Kari, who looks doubtful.

Janelle nods her head, looking pleased with herself.

"Well, at least we have a place to start," I say.

I close Jada's e-port and start walking upstairs to grab a bag to take with me. Kari follows right up the stairs with me.

"And what are you going to do then?" Kari asks. "Walk around aimlessly hoping she's just sitting there on the street? Think this through, Tobias! You can't go dragging a child on a dead-end trip like this! Jada could be anywhere!"

Ignoring her, I rush into my bedroom. I sink to my knees and lift up the bed skirt and dig around underneath.

Pushing aside the mass of clutter stuffed below our bed, my fingers finally make contact with what I'm searching for. Carefully, I pull out the box I bought the moment we moved here. I can feel Kari watching me from behind. She closes the bedroom door, as though knowing what it holds. Clicking open the small metal locks, I take out the Kel-Tec PF 9 pistol. It only has seven rounds. I pray I don't have to use a single one of them.

"Do you even know how to fire that thing?" Kari whispers.

Instead of answering, I load the magazine and stuff it in the back of my pants and kick the empty box back under the bed.

A second later there is a knock at the door.

Kari frowns at me before she opens it. Janelle walks in scratching her head and holding a new drawing.

"What does this mean, Papa?"

I kneel down and prepare myself to try and translate more scribbles, but this time, I know exactly what she's drawn. I take the pad out of her hands and into my own shaking ones. With wide eyes, I turn it around to show Kari.

$$\dagger \, \Gamma \, \phi$$

"He's got her in a frat house," I whisper, dropping the pad to the floor. Janelle scrambles to pick it back up, looking back at Kari and me for answers.

My mind starts to race. There used to be a university in Montmorency... I remember reading about it when we first moved here. The economy had forced its closure. It was a huge deal. Jada's work got a lot of their books when they went under. And most importantly, I know *exactly* where it is.

"Kari..." The look in my eyes must tell her everything.

"Go. I'll watch her. Be careful."

I scoop Janelle up in my arms and give her a huge hug.

"Are we going to get Mommy now?"

"I'm gonna go get her, peanut. Can you stay here and take care of Ms. Kari?"

She nods her head, excited at the idea of babysitting a grownup. "I'll go and get my babies!" she squeals, pushing out of my arms and running into her room.

"Keep your port on," I tell Kari. "I'll keep you updated."

Kari gives me a grim nod. I check the gun again and then run down the stairs.

I'm coming, Jada. I'm coming.

CHAPTER TWELVE

Jada

Over the sound of my sobs, I hear the distinct series of clicks at the front door as the latches release. The door opens, then quickly closes. A series of locks snapping shut echo inside the house.

For a moment, I'm consumed with absolute and utter hopelessness. After seeing firsthand what his tainted cologne does to me, I know his plan will work without flaw. Tobias will be crushed beyond repair. I can't allow that. I can't!

A surge of energy floods my body. This is the chance to escape, while he's gone. I use all my strength to pull hard against the ties. The hope is that by tugging on them, they will loosen up enough for me to get at least a hand free.

I plant my feet against the wall and lean my body back against the ties, praying they will weaken with the friction. The pain in my wrists is almost unbearable, but I twist against the restraints, pinching my eyes closed with the strain.

As I pull farther back against the wall, a small bit of warmth touches my skin. I open my eyes and peer down at my wrists in the crack of light coming in from under the door. Instantly, I know what the warmth is: blood—

my blood. The heat I felt a second ago was not from the friction on the ties, but from the scars on my wrists opening themselves up again.

The etching of my name and attempted suicide a few years ago has left the flesh along the area where the ties are seemingly more fragile than I would have guessed.

I'm bleeding, quite badly by the looks of it, tied up, and alone. Tears cascade along the edges of my scarred face. This is it. I'm going to bleed out right here in this prison he's made for me.

I sink down to my knees on the bed, watching helplessly as blood drips down my arms.

Perhaps this is for the best. Now Hawk won't be able to carry out his twisted plans for me. Maybe finding me dead on this bed will be some sort of poetic justice. Maybe he'll just run and leave Janelle and Tobias alone.

My head starts to feel dizzy. *Is this it? Is this the end?*

As my brain wages war with itself, I feel my tears begin to slow. *Think, Jada. Think. Just stop the bleeding.* This isn't like the time I cut myself in the woods, though. I won't be able to rip my shirt up to make a tourniquet. Not tied up like this. Or can I? Looking down at the pale-yellow sheet on the bed, my brain switches itself into survival mode.

Using my feet, I kick and pull against the sheet with the tips of my toes. At first, the fabric doesn't give, but once one side slips off the corner, a second quickly follows suit. As quickly as I can, I scrape the sides of my feet against the loose fabric until all sides are free.

It takes quite a bit of effort and strain, but I manage to work the sheet into a sort of blob. Using my head I'm able to inch the blob up the wall until my fingers can grab hold.

Balling the fabric together in my bound hands, I place it over my wrists. I have to use my head to apply pressure to my cuts, but it's the only option I have.

The fabric stings against the fresh gashes. I bite against my lip to stop myself from passing out. I press my head against my wrists as hard as I can in an effort to stay alive.

Exhausted from the effort of getting the sheet off the damn bed, I take several large gulps of air as I try to steady my heart rate. I need to calm down so the blood doesn't pump as fast.

I close my eyes against the throbbing in my wrists and wait for Hawk to come back and cut me free.

I realize, of course, that it's ironic that I'm praying for Hawk and not Tobias, but I know the reality of where I am. Tobias will never find me here because Hawk wanted it that way. The only thing I can hope to wish for is that the monster returns soon and decides he wants to help me.

Tobias

I fly down the stairwell of the apartment with renewed determination. I know where they are now. All I need to do is get there. If I plan this out right, Jada could be in my arms within the hour.

Once I'm out on the street, I scan the road for cabs, but of course, there isn't a single one in sight. Cursing, I head across the street toward the Metro line. I'll take the train, just as they did. It'll probably be faster than a cab anyway.

The two-block walk to the station is nothing but a blur of faces. Bits of conversations in French and English mix inside my head as my feet pull me forward. That's how I know I'm on the right path. It's as though my body is taking over now, being pulled in by the force of her now that I am within her orbit.

The sounds of the city fade into the distance and are soon replaced with dark echoes of conversations all around, the squeal of air breaks, and overhead announcements. The air is markedly thicker down here, but so far my lungs are holding out just fine. It's because I'm close. I just know it.

In the shadows of the tunnel, I wait impatiently for the train to arrive. Normally, I don't the take the Metro. I have so little patience waiting around for trains and buses that I'd rather just walk to my destination. Unfortunately, Montmorency is too far, even for a healthy person.

I start to pace across the gray brick-lined station floor. The subways here are by far much cleaner than those in the States. I'm hard pressed to find even a dried-up wad of gum on these well-kept floors.

Every few seconds that I pace, I lean over the side to check the tunnel for the twin beams of light to come. All that greets me is the darkness of the Metro tunnel made darker by the years of exhaust fumes. Although the surfaces are clean, *that* is a smell I can almost taste. Asthma can do that to you, make you taste pollutants. It's nasty. No one likes the taste of exhaust.

To either side of me, more passengers start to arrive.

They, too, begin the pace of impatience as they lose calls and their connections drop in the depths of the tunnel. Those that came before me are now reaching my level of frustration and we exchange mutual glances of shared annoyance.

I look up again at the time displayed on the screen overhead: 10:12. *The train should have been here four minutes ago!*

My pacing becomes more labored as I begin debating taking the bus instead. The bus lines are notoriously slow, but at this rate, they may be faster. Heck, I might even be able to find a cab now.

Resolved, my feet turn toward the stairs when a series of four beeps sound from overhead, indicating an incoming message to passengers.

"Attention passengers: Due to a mechanical malfunction, the northbound line will be delayed. It is unknown how long the repair will take. Please seek alternate transportation until further notice."

Groans fill the air around me, but none as deep as the one I make.

Of course!

All at once, there is a mad dash to the stairs as people rush to get to the cabs and buses above ground. I curse under my breath. *Why didn't I leave earlier?* Now nothing will be available!

The commuter train won't run again until 11:00, so I'll have to try my luck on the bus line along with everyone else. By the time I get up there, any cabs will be long gone.

Angry at myself for not leaving sooner, I try to push past the mob that's crowding the exit. Bodies slowly merge back up the stairs. A large man wearing a pink Hawaiian shirt, of all things, is in front of me, talking to some dude in a ball cap. He's taking his sweet time climbing the steps, so I try to duck my way through the narrow opening between them.

I'm almost past them when a thick hand grabs my arm, forcing me down the step I'd just climbed.

"Didn't your mama teach you any manners, boy," the man says, sneering at me. Beside him, baseball hat laughs, urging him on. Although the guy towers over me by nearly a foot and easily outweighs me, I'm in no mood for this. I need to find Jada.

"Get your hand off me," I warn.

"Or what, jackass?" He laughs, shoving me into the person behind me, who gives me a shove of his own.

Ticked off, I climb the stairs, keeping my focus on Mr. Hawaiian shirt. As soon as we've cleared the top stair and the crowd thins, I do something stupid and childish. I steamroll Hawaiian shirt as hard as I can, catching him off guard. I hear him grunt as my body makes contact with him. He goes flying forward as I brush past. My shoulder throbs a bit from the contact, but I don't even stop to look back, and I should have.

Just as I'm about to take another step, his fist makes an upper cut to my side, my *left* side. Intense pain fills my already strained lung.

The deserved blow sinks me to the ground, while the pair laughs at me. They walk off muttering, "That'll teach him."

As I wheeze and struggle to catch my breath, I can't

help but notice that not a single person is stopping to check to see if I'm all right. They're all too wrapped up in their own problems and conversations to notice some poor kid wheezing on the Metro floor. Karma truly is a bitch.

I manage to work my way over to a bench after the crowd departs. Of course, I'd left the apartment in such a rush that I didn't think to grab my inhaler. *Idiot!*

Collapsing against the bench, I sink down onto my back and breathe as slowly as I can.

Hang on, Jada. Please, hang on.

Hawk

These last few pills won't seem to sell. I've been walking around Montreal for the last hour and a half and I've been able to get rid of all but these six. I didn't get as much as I'd hoped. Cheap bastards. I debate trying the other side of town to check out my prospects, but Seth starts in about wasting time.

Save the drugs. You may need them if Jada doesn't behave.

"Shut up." I spit, kicking at the ground. I'm not going to need any more than the batch I made. That will last me until we get settled. Once she sees how much better off she is with me and how good I'm going to treat her, she won't need to be drugged into thinking she loves me, because she just will.

But what if she doesn't?

"I told you to shut up!"

My voice echoes down the empty street. A dog barks somewhere in the distance, a painful reminder that I'm talking to myself.

"Fine," I mutter. I'll save these few but only to sell later. I won't need them for Jada. She loves me. She's just too messed up to know it. I'll just proceed with the plan. Everything will be fine.

With some of the cash I got from the sales, I head to the nearest Metro and make my way back to the frat house. Once I'm close, I'll pick up what we need for the next stage of the plan at a corner store.

"Soon, baby. This will all be over soon."

CHAPTER THIRTEEN

Jada

I've lost all sense of time since I've been here. Either that or I've lost too much blood. It feels like it's been days since Hawk left, but it may have only been minutes. I have no way of knowing. The room is so dark that it's hard to judge the time. It seems like it's still daylight, but maybe I'm imagining it?

I think the bleeding may have stopped, but I'm too scared to take the pressure off my wrists. Actually, I don't want to see the blood again. I pride myself on the fact that I haven't wanted to cut again for these last few years, but after seeing those wounds sliced open again... they only reminded me of the weak and tormented girl I had been before Janelle came into my life, and right now I need all the strength I can get. I can't allow myself to sink back into that depression. Not now.

Tobias is the only person who has ever seen past my scars and into the woman I dreamed I could be. He saw through my tough girl act and the broken girl I actually was and loved me anyway.

After everything we've been through to find each

other, *this* is how it was going to end? What was it all for, all of our suffering, all of our agony, if I'm just going to die anyway?

"Honey, I'm home!" Hawk's voice sings against the darkness.

I can't help the relief I feel upon hearing his voice. I cry out to Hawk for help.

The sound of something loud being dropped echoes in the darkness, and then his footsteps come.

"Jada?"

A second later, he kicks open the bedroom door, his breathing labored. He takes one look at me and my hunched-over body and bloodied sheet and grows pale.

"Jada, Jesus Christ! What the hell did you *do*?"

He rushes over to my bed and gently lifts my head off the sheet, exposing the blood that has soaked through it.

"I'm sorry," I whimper. *God, why am I apologizing to him?* "My scars must have opened up against the strain of the ties. I couldn't stop the bleeding… I didn't know what else to do…"

For a moment he just stares at me. Then his lips form a hard line. A look of determination takes hold of him. Without a word, he disappears out of the room.

"Hawk, please, come back!" I wail. "Hawk!"

The outside door opens again and slams behind him.

I sit on the bed, awestruck. *Is he just going to leave me here?* My body slumps. Maybe I am going to die here. Alone and tied to this bed. Maybe he's just realized I wasn't worth all this trouble.

A second later, however, he reappears with what looks like a bunch of wildflowers and his knife. For half a minute I think he's just going to kill me now and cut his losses, but he sinks down to the bed and looks me in the eyes. I can see the worry etched in them. In that moment, I forget the monster that kidnapped me. Instead, I see the best friend Tobias grew up with. The boy that never got the affection he deserved from his own family. For one second, I feel sorry for Hawk. Angry even that he's cursed with an illness that is so clearly raging inside his mind.

When he looks away, my fears return. He grabs the knife and brings it up to me. I shrink back, but he holds me still. With skilled hands he slices open the ties. The relief of the plastic no longer cutting into my flesh makes me begin to sob. Hawk looks down at me as though realizing what he's done to me and pulls me into his arms.

"I'm so sorry," he whispers into my ear. "I never even thought about your scars. That was so stupid of me."

He drops his hands from me and without warning starts hitting his head with his hands, repeatedly. And hard. He balls his hands into fists and beats himself with them over and over against the side of his skull. I can actually hear his knuckles cracking from the impact against his head.

That's when the screaming begins. He starts yelling at some unseen demon as he appears to punish himself. It is absolutely terrifying. Although still weak from blood loss, I back away from him, scared about what he's doing to himself, what he could do to me if I got too close.

"You're so stupid, Hawk! No wonder she doesn't

love you! Shut up! She does love me! You don't know what you're talking about! You're gonna screw this whole thing up!"

As Hawk writhes beside me, I realize this would be the perfect time to escape. I have no idea how long an attack of the mind like this would take, so if I want to try, it had better be now.

With my heart in my throat, I throw a leg over the bed. When he doesn't notice, I start to draw my other leg over. That's when he lets out such a guttural scream that I freeze.

In the next moment, he grabs hold of my thigh. The pads of his fingers dig deep into my flesh, causing me to release a scream of my own. In a flash, his wild eyes return to their menacing calm.

"See?" Hawk tells me. "I don't need pills. I got this under control."

Panting, I look carefully at him.

"Hawk... what's going on with you?" I can't help it. My damn sympathetic heart can't risk trying to help him. "Why did you just hit yourself? Who thinks you're stupid? Please, Hawk, if you're sick, let me help you."

He throws me a deadly glare, but I will myself to speak again.

"Hawk, I know what it's like—to hate yourself."

I risk a tentative touch on his shoulder. I'm hoping against hope that I can appeal to his kinder side. A side I know still lingers in there—somewhere. Maybe he just needs someone to help him? Maybe he just needs someone to tell him things will be okay... Maybe he just needs someone to care about him? I, for one, know what feeling alone and unloved can do to a person.

His snort, however, doesn't bode well for my theory. "I don't hate myself." He pushes my hand off his shoulder but keeps the vise grip on my leg.

"That prison doc thinks I have schizophrenia." He laughs at a spot on the floor that seems to be taunting him. "I'm not crazy!" he shouts at the spot.

Afraid to even breathe, I stay frozen in place.

After a few blinks of his lids, however, he seems almost human again. "Let's get you cleaned up." He smiles down at me as though nothing happened.

Before I can say anything, he scoops me up in his arms gently and brings me out into the living room. I don't struggle in his arms this time. I don't dare. After the transformation I just saw, I'm even more terrified of Hawk than I had been before. If he is schizophrenic and not taking his meds, there's no telling what his paranoia might make him do.

He plops me down onto the couch and I don't move. He drags the now-empty end table closer to me and lays his knife on it. For half a second, I contemplate going for it, but before the thought can take root, he's brought the flowers he gathered a moment ago and puts them down to the table. Using the edge of the blade, he starts pressing against the small yellow buds.

"What are you doing?"

He doesn't look up from his work but keeps pressing the flowers into a pile of mush.

"It's yarrow. I grabbed some from the side of the house. It'll help make sure your wounds clot."

"Yarrow? How did you know that?"

He stops pressing the leaves and looks up at me.

"The woods are my home, Jada. I know their secrets.

I told you. I'll keep you safe once we're there." He goes back to mashing up the flowers until he's formed a yellowish paste.

Scooping the mess up with the edge of the knife, he brings it over to my cut and gently places a wad of it on one of the gashes. I expect it to hurt, but it just feels cool against my flesh.

"Hold it," he says as he pulls off his shirt. I dart my eyes to the ground, not wanting to look at his exposed chest.

He grabs the knife and starts to slit his shirt into strips. When he has several slices, he carefully removes my hand from the paste and places a few strips of cloth around the yarrow. With a third strip, he ties it together, then does the same with my other hand. He is surprisingly tender and gentle with me, but I'm not quick to forget how he behaved a moment ago.

As he works, I take a quick glance around the room. I notice the windows are still covered, betraying the real time of day. A large brown grocery bag is sprawled out on the floor where he dropped it. Some of the contents have spilled and lie in a heap on the ground. I can make out a loaf of bread and a box of hair dye.

When he finishes with the bandages, my wrists feel surprisingly better. That's when he pulls the ties out of his pocket. It's my turn to go crazy. *He can't honestly want to put me back in those!*

"Shh, it's okay. I'm not going to do your hands, I promise." He reaches out and snags my leg and whips a tie around it before I can stop him. I yank my other leg underneath my body, trying to keep it free.

"Jada, stop fighting me on this so I can get you

cleaned up!"

I don't stop, though. I can't be bound up again like an animal. I can't. I use all my weight to push against him, but I'm weak from blood loss and he's got leverage on his side and easily pins my arms to the couch. He's careful not to grab my wrists, but I still buck underneath him.

"Damn it, Jada! I said stop." He reaches for something over the couch, releasing my hands, which I use to beat against his chest. I only manage to get in a few blows before he comes at my face with the something. It looks like a perfume bottle.

That's the stuff he used on me before!

I scream under him as he sprays his chest with the mist. He tosses the bottle aside and stifles my scream with his hand.

Muffled cries escape his fingers.

"When I release my hand, you're going to breathe this in and be a good girl. Got it?"

He removes his hand and I pinch my lips together, pathetically trying to hold my breath. Strong hands hold me in place as he waits for me to succumb to the need for air.

After a few moments, my lips part and I inhale great gulps of poisoned air. Maybe this time I can resist the drug now that I know what it's doing to me. Maybe I can—nope.

I feel my mind slip. The muscles in my body loosen. A big goofy grin spreads across my lips.

"Hi," I purr.

"Now that's more like it," Hawk says, letting my arms go.

"Do we get to play now?" My hands reach out to touch him, but he stops me. I pout.

"We need to get you cleaned up first. I can't risk you getting an infection. No hospitals." He takes my arm and kisses it so gently that I want to cry. He's so kind to me.

Hawk picks me up and carries me into the kitchen, my head pressed snugly against his firm bicep.

He sets me down on the counter where he tries to let go of me, but I hold on to him, wanting to smother him with kisses. I manage to get a few in before he slips a few inches out of my grasp. From a bag that rests on the counter beside me, he snags a roll of paper towels still wrapped in plastic and a bowl from a cabinet. He then grabs a bagged water from the twelve-pack on the counter.

After he's cleaned the dust that's caked on the bowl from years of disuse, he takes my arm and positions it over the metal rim. Slowly, he dumps about half of the bottle over my arm. I flinch as I watch dried-up blood vanish and tinge the bowl pink. Looking at the water laced with my blood brings back the oddest sense of déjà vu, but I can't recall why.

I don't shrink away when he starts to rub away the blood that's clotted near the bandages. The pain is tolerable as long as he's beside me. I breathe in his heady scent, wondering if my life could be any better than in this moment with Hawk.

Tobias

It's almost ten thirty now and I haven't even made it out of the Metro station!

My stupid lungs are having the hardest time staying full. Every time I think I'm okay, I try to get up, only to have the familiar burn for air return.

Jada is counting on me and here I am, flat on my ass all because I was a prick!

Furious with myself, I decide to try and make small jaunts to the bus line. If I can make a few feet at a time and then rest, at least I'm making progress. Sitting here doing nothing is not an option.

While I inch my way along the wall, I try to formulate my plan of attack once I finally get there. At this point, all I have is getting to the campus and hoping to magically find the frat sign Janelle drew. Beyond that, I have no idea what to do. I have a sneaking suspicion, though, that it's going to involve the loaded pistol resting snuggly against the crook of my back.

When push comes to shove, though, do I honestly think I'll be able to pull the trigger on Hawk? He was my best friend for seventeen years...

I guess my mind will be made up for me depending on what state I found Jada in. If he's hurt her, there's no way he's coming out of this alive.

With that thought lodged firmly into my head, I push my way farther along the wall.

CHAPTER FOURTEEN

Jada

I continue to gaze at Hawk's face as he removes the bandages from my arm, gently dabbing at the marks on my wrists with the wet paper towel.

The blood gives way to what looks like letters. My name. *Huh? I have scars of my name on my forearm. Weird.* I don't remember that? It seems like I should remember that. Trying to recall how it got there, I feel my memories shift inside my head. It's kinda like I'm underwater, floating around. It's not like drowning, though. This feeling I'm having... it's warm and relaxing. I never want it to stop.

"Okay," Hawk says, "I think you're good now. The yarrow helped you clot up nicely, but I'm gonna keep the bandages on. Just in case." He proceeds to wrap me back up as I run my fingers over his as they work.

"You should probably have some food too." He scratches his head. "Don't they make you eat after you give blood?"

I giggle and shrug my shoulders.

Walking back over to the grocery bag, he pulls out a candy bar and tosses it to me.

Suddenly ravished, I tear into the wrapper and sink

my teeth into its caramel center. Heaven. As I munch, he takes the rest of the contents out of the bag.

He removes two touristy T-shirts that say "Montreal" in bold print. Then he digs out a second carton of hair dye and a pair of bright-yellow rubber gloves.

"Cool. Are we dying our hair?" I ask, running my fingers through my hair.

"Yup. We're going black."

"Mmm, I bet you're gonna look sexy in black."

"You're gonna be the sexy one. I'm not gonna be able to keep my hands off you." Something in my stomach flutters, and it doesn't feel like desire.

What is that feeling?

I push the thought aside as Hawk leads me back into the living room where he drags a folding chair over to the couch and straddles it. He hands me the box and the gloves.

"Have fun," he says.

Cocking my head to the side, I smile, put down the candy bar, and tear the box open and pull out the first bottle.

"You know I don't know what I'm doing, right?" I laugh at him.

"It's easy. Just mix the two foam bottles together and use the brush thingy to put it on my hair."

"You've dyed your hair before?"

He looks over his shoulder at me. "No. But I read the instructions. Let's go. We're on a tight schedule."

"Yes, sir." I laugh, saluting him.

Giddy for no reason, I unscrew both bottles, per the instructions on the box, and pour them in the small bowl provided. The smell of the two chemicals mixing together is intense. It stings my nose and makes my eyes water. Instinctively, my head pulls away from the foul smell. Then, without warning, an overwhelming urge to actually go back and smell the mixture floods over me.

Smell the dye, a voice inside my head whispers.

At first I resist, but the voice grows louder. Curious, I lower my face to the bowl and inhale—deeply. Without warning, my head spins from the fumes. I reel back trying to get the smell out of my nose. Tiny stars dance in my eyes, but I bend over and smell the dye again.

Even though the scent is nauseating, I can think clearer. My head is killing me, but instantly, I know what the dye is doing. The scent of the toxins is overpowering Hawk's poison.

My head pops up, and I check to see if he noticed my reaction. His hand is currently scratching the back of his head and his gaze is at his feet. He doesn't know.

Testing the air, I bring the bowl away from me. I feel like myself, but there is definitely a connection to this chemical reaction.

Standing beside my captor, I notice my hands and feet are unbound. One thought flashes across my mind: *RUN!*

My eyes flick back to check on Hawk. His body is turning up to look at me. In that moment, I realize I have to keep up my act. Keep pretending. Come up with a plan.

"This looks gross," I say, stirring around my saving grace. My heart thunders against my chest, and I wonder suddenly if he can hear it.

"Yeah, well, hurry up and put it in already."

I snap to attention, knowing I need to play this card right. It's the only one I'll be dealt.

"Right," I say, trying to sound casual. With shaky fingers, I put the brush into the bowl. A thick blob of the mix adheres itself to the nylon bristles. Slowly, I lift the brush and stroke it through the back of his hair. Dark paste begins to cover his scalp.

My whole body trembles with fear, wondering just how long I can keep up this charade before he discovers the truth. What if he tries to kiss me or touch me? I'll never be able to tolerate it. He'll figure it out. He'll tie me up again.

No. This is my chance. I have to think logically. As I work the dye along the sides of his head, I sneak in tentative glances around the room, looking for exits.

The front door is closest, but there are at least three locks on it. Fumbling with locks would take time, time I know Hawk wouldn't afford me.

To my left is the kitchen. No viable exits there. Behind me are the two bedrooms: one that I'd been held in and the other that has a door slightly ajar. Those would both be dead ends. Along the far wall is a stairwell leading upstairs with more dead ends. Which means my best option for escape is, unfortunately, the front door—and managing those locks. I bite my lip and gather more dye, inhaling deeply as I place a large dollop on the top of his head.

I'll need to find a way to get time alone. Even a minute could work.

Applying the last of the solution onto Hawk's head, I hear myself ask what may be the key to my escape: "How long do you need to leave this in before you wash it out?"

When he goes to rinse his head off, it might be just the chance I need. While he's busy rinsing I could be busy unlocking. All I need to do is play it cool until then.

"What does the box say?"

Steadying my hand, I put down the applicator brush and pick up the box and try to focus on the words.

"Twenty minutes."

Twenty minutes. Assuming I could keep the lie up that long, I might have a chance. Hope dances in my heart.

"Okay. Your turn," Hawk says, getting up out of the chair. He stretches his arms over his head, showing off his lean body. It reminds me just how powerful he is.

As he gestures for me to take the seat, I do my best not to look as shocked as I actually am. I'd forgotten I need to dye my hair too. For some reason I assumed we would wait to see how his came out before we did mine, but looking back on it, why would he wait? He wants us out of here. Time is against us.

Keeping my telltale eyes to the floor, I slide into the hardness of the chair. My muscles scream from all the bruises and pulled muscles I've sustained, but I have to pretend none of it affects me, that I'm happy to be here with him. I grip my hands against the edge of the wood and try to keep the tension from showing in my shoulders.

Once I've leaned back against the chair, he runs his hands through my tangled hair. I have to stop myself from flinching at his touch. Instead, I let out a soft moan and hope to hell it sounds like I'm enjoying his touch instead of wanting to throttle him.

"I hate that I have to cover up your beautiful hair, but it's only temporary. Once we're safely in the woods, we can go back to our natural colors."

If my plan of escape fails and he gets us out of the country, I realize I'll need to try to find a way to communicate his plans to Tobias. *But how?* It's not like I can just grab a scrap of paper and jot down Hawk's maniacal plan.

My eyes drift around the room as Hawk continues to play with my hair.

The only thing even close to me is the end table that holds the second unopened box of dye. That won't help... or will it? Glancing at it again, I notice it has a lower shelf. A shelf covered in dust. I could write something in the dust...

Biting my lip, I wait for Hawk to open the box. I'll have to be discrete.

"I've never been a big outdoors person, but I'm sure you'll make it fun," I say, trying to be girly. As I talk, I lower my hand and draw a picture of a tent in the dust. I'm trying to look cute, making a childish drawing, hoping he doesn't pick up on what I'm actually doing.

"You're going to love it. I can make us enough money to get some good gear too, once the drug money is gone. Skins are worth a lot and I know how to bag an animal without damaging the best parts of the fur."

That image does little to make me feel any better.

"It gets pretty cold out at night, though, doesn't it?" I ask, keeping my voice as light as I can.

His face slinks down to my ear. "I'll keep you warm, baby, don't you worry."

I clench my teeth together and force a smile.

"Besides," he continues, standing back up and mixing the solution again, "I'm thinking we could head some place warm... maybe the Carolinas or something. We'll figure it out. We've got nothing but time now."

My stomach reels with the idea of us out in the woods with him. Janelle would be terrified out in the dark at night. All the more reason my escape *has* to work. He's not going to lay a finger on my daughter.

"We'll be happy there, Jada. I promise. We'll finally be a family."

I swallow down the lump in my throat, but I have to contain myself.

"Mmm," is all I can manage.

Surprising me, he drops the bowl on the table and rounds the corner of the chair and kneels down in front of me. His piercing blue eyes lock me in place.

"I'm going to make you happy, Jada. I promise."

Unavoidable tears run from the corners of my eyes.

Mistaking them for tears of joy, he catches one with the pad of his thumb and licks it off. "I love you, Jada. So much."

His lips crash down onto mine before I can even register the movement. I will myself to melt into his kiss. I conjure up every image of Tobias that I can to make the façade work. Holding back the bile, I wrap my arms around him and pull him closer. When his tongue worms its way into my mouth, I have to force myself not to bite it off.

Tobias

By the time I finally get onto a bus, I'm beyond winded. It's been over an hour just trying to get my butt in this seat. My lungs are burning and I need my inhaler, but I can't stop until I've found Jada. I just can't. Not when she's this close.

The bus bumps and thrusts itself down the road while I try to slow my breathing. I need to be at my best once I get off this rig. *Why didn't I bring my inhaler!*

Taking out Jada's e-port, I message Kari that I'm on the bus and will let her know when I find them. *If I find them.*

Her reply back comes faster than I expect.

"Which bus are you on?" her reply reads.

"#12," I type. "Getting off at Montmorency in a few."

I'm just about to shove the screen back in when a second message comes across.

"Good. I'm there now. Been waiting for you forever. I'll explain when you get here."

What? Kari's at the bus stop? I try to send her a message back, but the screen goes black. The battery just died. *Of course.*

What is going on? Why is Kari at the Montmorency stop? And why would she drag Janelle with her? Kari's the one who told me taking Janelle was reckless, and of course, after I calmed down, I completely agreed. So what happened to make her change her mind and risk bringing my daughter into this?

A cycle of scenarios rages in my head, and none of them are good. One thing is for sure, Kari is going to get Janelle out of here. I am not risking her safety. No way in hell.

CHAPTER FIFTEEN

Tobias

When the bus finally arrives, I see Kari wringing her hands together and pacing. My eyes dart immediately to the bench beside her. Janelle isn't anywhere in sight. In that second, my worst fears dance inside my head. *Hawk has my daughter.*

The second the doors open, I start my attack.

"Where is Janelle?" I shout at her.

Kari shrinks back against my tone but frowns a second later.

"Calm down, she's fine. She's with your neighbor."

"Ms. Skillings? Why?" The bus pulls away from the curb, its loud engine drowning out parts of my rant. "Why is she there, Kari? I left her with you because I knew she'd be safe with you! What if Hawk comes back for her? You don't think when no one answers his knock he'll just walk away, do you? He'll find her, Kari. You have to go back. You have to get Janelle and take her somewhere. Anywhere! Just get her out of that apartment until I contact you!"

Kari stands calmly beside me as my face grows red with rage. Of course, all that yelling has left me in even worse shape than I was. I clap a hand to my chest, willing my lungs to calm down.

She sighs at my overexerted condition and takes my arm. She leads me over to a bench just under a willow tree and makes me sit. As I struggle with my breathing, Kari looks over her shoulder, as though to make sure no one's listening.

"Tobias, I know you're flying off the handle right now, but you need to calm down and listen to what I have to say."

Clenching my fists in frustration, I say, "Talk fast."

Kari lets out a quick exhalation before she begins.

"After you left, Janelle started… talking funny."

My body tenses at her expression. She *has* been saying some pretty spooky things lately. "Funny how?"

Kari's face scrunches up. "I don't know how to explain this without sounding crazy."

"Just tell me!"

"Okay, calm down. After you left, Janelle went over to the window to watch you leave, but then she closed her eyes for a long time. I thought for a moment that she'd gone off and fallen asleep on me, but then she popped her eyes open and she started talking, only—it wasn't her voice, Tobias."

"What are you talking about?" I ask.

She blows air out of her mouth and bites the edge of her lip. "This is where the crazy part begins. You remember Naya and Etash?"

I cock my head to the side. Why is she asking about them? What do they have to do with anything? They died years ago, but I humor her with the information she wants me to tell her.

"Yeah?"

Kari rubs her eyes. "The night they died… I was at

160

the ER. They were still working on Etash, hoping they could bring him back. He'd been stabbed in the lung. His *left* lung."

"So?"

"And it just so happens that your left lung is diseased."

"What are you trying to say, Kari? That the reason my lung is infected is because some kid got knifed in his lung?"

Her eyes tell me that is, indeed, what she's trying to say.

"You don't think it's more than just a coincidence that the night he died from a puncture to his left lung, you show up on this earth with a problem in your left lung not two seconds after he died?"

"Okay, I'll admit the idea is creepy, but what does that have to do with finding Jada!" I know I'm shouting, but I don't understand where this is going. We're wasting time! Time Jada might not have.

Kari wrings her hands again. A strand of her graying hair falls across her face, catching against her lip, a lip that is now trembling. "I know this doesn't seem important right now, and maybe it isn't, but maybe it's everything. I just don't know!" She throws her hands up in the air and takes a few steps away from me.

Something tells me to cut her some slack and listen to why she came out here.

"I'm sorry, Kari," I say. "I'm just kinda going out of my mind over here. Finish your story. If it will help find Jada, then I need to know what's going on."

Kari's forehead wrinkles with concern, but she begins again.

"Okay. While they were still trying to save Etash in the hospital, I was in the ER, waiting for some bit of good news from all of it. My best friend had already died a few minutes earlier, but I held out hope that Etash would make it." Her eyes overflowed with tears, and I suddenly felt like a jerk for not being more sympathetic earlier.

"While I was bawling my head off, still reeling from it all, an elderly woman came and sat beside me. It was Etash's grandmother. His whole family was there, praying and crying. It was awful." Kari wipes away a few of the tears from her face. "Anyway, his grandmother was from India or somewhere because she had this thick accent. She told me she had the gift to see the future. I thought she was nuts, but I let her talk because it seemed like she needed to tell me something." Kari paused as though trying to pull herself together. "She told me that her grandson was gone from this world, but he would be reborn. She said Naya would be too, and that their love would help them find each other again. I smiled and nodded, but I didn't believe her. A few seconds after she told me this, the docs came out to let Etash's family know he'd passed away."

She paused to take some great gulps of air. I didn't want to be insensitive, but I didn't see what this had to do with anything.

"I'm not trying to be an ass, but why are you mentioning Etash's grandmother?" I say the words carefully, afraid I might set her off.

"Because when your daughter finally opened her eyes and spoke, it was with the voice of Etash's grandmother. Even though I heard it years ago, I would recognize that accent anywhere."

I gape at her, my mouth partially open.

"You want me to believe that my daughter is possessed by Etash's grandmother?" The disbelief in my voice is thick, but I don't care. This is insane.

I stand up from the bench and glare at Kari.

"It's more than that, Tobias. I think Janelle is the grandmother, reincarnated. I did a search. His grandmother passed away on Janelle's birthday."

I can't help it, but my eyes widen at the idea.

"There's more. She had this in her hand." She holds out a small pendant. It looks like some sort of a yin-yang symbol, but instead of one side being white and the other being black, both the sides are covered in flames. One side is covered with a blue flame and the other side is orange flames.

"What is that?" I ask, running my finger over the sliver edges.

"That is a pendant his grandmother gave me. She told me she'd wanted to give it to Etash since he'd found his Twin Flame, but since he and his Flame had passed, she was giving it to me. She knew I would find its rightful owner one day."

I look up from the pendant to Kari. Her face is white.

"Tobias, I lost that pendant years ago."

It's my turn to go pale. "Then how did Janelle...?"

"I don't know," Kari whispers.

My head spins as I try to absorb all of this.

"What did Janelle say to you... when she spoke in the strange accent?"

My heart rate accelerates waiting for her to answer.

"She told me I needed to find you. She said you'd be here, at this bus stop. She's the one who told me to leave her with Ms. Skillings. She said it was imperative that I be with you or all would be lost."

My limited source of air becomes thinner, and I start to cough despite my desire not to.

Kari suddenly blinks as though she's remembering something. She rushes to her bag, digging around for something. "Janelle also said I needed to bring you this." She opens her hand to reveal my inhaler.

I look from the inhaler to the look in Kari's eyes. She's scared by what she heard my daughter say, and after everything I've heard today, so am I.

Slowly, I reach out with trembling fingers and take it. *How did she know I was going to need this?*

Popping off the top, I take in the healing mist, allowing it to coat my lungs. After a few inhalations, my lungs are allowed to expand. The burning subsides to just a memory far faster than normal. After an attack like this, I should be flat on my back with my mask on for at least a day, but I'm feeling remarkably strong.

"Did Janelle tell you anything else?"

"Just that we need to find the building with that sign she drew. And that we need to hurry. Jada doesn't have much time left."

Listening to the advice of an apparently reincarnated Indian woman, I push up off the bench. My nostrils flare with a new-found fury and we set off together to find Jada.

CHAPTER SIXTEEN

Jada

The smell of the dye in his hair as he thrusts his tongue in my mouth overpowers the spray on his chest, which keeps me lucid and nauseated at the same time. After several sloppy kisses, he finally removes his lips from mine and I plaster on a smile. Satisfied with himself, he goes back to the task at hand: camouflaging me for my kidnapping.

"Once your hair is done, I'll go and get Janelle, but don't worry, I won't dye her hair. We can just cut it short and dress her like a boy to throw any onlookers off our tail."

I bite my lip hard to keep from screaming at him to leave my daughter out of this.

Hawk sighs, contented. "Our new life will start tomorrow," he says, brushing his fingers against the line of my scar. I force myself to lean into his hand and not shrink away.

"I'll find a way to fix your face too. I'll make everything better, Jada. You'll see."

I swallow the lump that's lodged in my throat. Time is running out. If my escape doesn't work... No. It is going to work. It has to.

Hawk kisses my cheek gently before he finally lets go of my hands and buries them into my hair instead. After a moment, he tells my blond good-bye.

Behind me, he starts to prepare the dye. The chemicals mix together; their overpowering scent fuels the need to finish the task at hand. I glance over my shoulder to watch him work, trying to be seductive.

While he stirs, his expression shifts. His eyebrows crinkle. He cocks his head to the side, looking at me. Panic begins. Slowly, he sniffs the air. He stirs the mixture a few more times, then lowers his nose to the bowl. *Shit!* When his jaw hardens, I know he's piecing it together. His eyes narrow on the bowl. He takes another inhalation and turns to look at me, making me cold.

"What's wrong?" I ask, trying to keep up the failing act.

"Tell me you love me." His words are slow. Methodical. Fierce.

"What?"

He drops the bowl and is in front of me in a second. Yanking out a plastic tie from his back pocket, he waves it in my face.

"I said tell me you love me."

My heart beats frantically in my chest.

"I—I love you," I whisper, but the smallness of my voice betrays me.

He snarls at me. "You little wench. You thought you were gonna trick me, didn't you?"

"I don't know what you're talking about," I sputter, pushing my body hard against the chair.

"Don't lie to me!" he screams. The veins in his

forehead throb against his flesh, showing the fullness of his rage.

Foolishly, I try to make a run for it, but he lunges for my hands the second my butt leaves the chair, anchoring me in place. Tears begin to fall down my face as I struggle against his weight. He pushes me back into the chair with his knee.

I'm rendered helpless, and he yanks my hands behind my back and locks my fists in place. He leans hard against my chest as his hands work blindly to fasten my wrists to the dowels of the chair.

"Hawk, stop, please!" I cry, but he grabs my face in his hand and holds me still.

"I should kill you right now for that."

His face blurs behind my tears.

"Then do it," I cry. Death would be better than being caged again.

"Shut up and let me think!" he shouts at me.

He sinks to his knees to bind my feet too, but not before I get in a few good kicks.

When he's locked me down, my body begins to convulse. My plan has failed. I'm stuck here for as long as he wants me to be.

Hawk

I told you she didn't love you. She's been playing you for a fool! You can't let her get away with that. You need to punish her, Hawk! Make her suffer! Make her love us!

"Argh! I was so *stupid*!" I kick the table beside me. It flies across the room and splinters against the wall as it breaks apart. "You thought you could play me, didn't you? Well, guess what? I'm smarter than you are. You're mine, Jada, and you're never going to leave me. Do you understand? Never!"

That's it! Make her fear us!

"Shut up! I can handle this!" I say, kicking at the couch as I pace.

I will not let Seth tell me what to do. I don't need his advice and I don't want him in my head.

Let me help you tame her!

His voice is screaming in my head and I just want him to stop. Tearing at my hair, I scream again, hoping he'll just go away.

You can't ignore me, Hawk. I'm part of you. The strong part. The part that Jada wants. No wonder she coils away from you. You're pathetic, a weakling. Jada needs a real man. She needs me.

"No!" I shout, laying my fist through the drywall. Immediately, I feel blood pooling along my knuckles, but I don't remove my hand. In that instant, Seth isn't in my head. It's quiet, and I don't dare move.

Feel better now? his voice taunts.

I rip my hand out of the wall, wishing I could rip this thing out of my head instead.

Across the room, Jada stares at me. I can see it in her eyes. She thinks I'm weak. Just like Seth said. Just like my parents thought. I'll show her who is in control here. I'll show them all!

"I tried to do this the easy way, Jada. But now you've left me with no choice."

Marching past her, I go into the kitchen and dump a few bottles of water over my head to get rid of the dye. I can't risk her not being in my full control, which means the dye needs to go.

Great pools of darkness cover my once-white tee as the color rinses out of my hair. I cross through the living room as the water drips down my chest like giant spider webs. When I reach the front door, I open it.

"What are you doing?" she yelps.

"Getting that stench out of here so it doesn't ruin the rest of my plan. You think you're so smart, Jada, but you'll see. I'll make you understand. You should never underestimate me."

As fresh air circulates into the room, I dig around in the bag for the T-shirts I bought for our disguise. I pull the stupid tourist shirt over my wet head. We're leaving today, damn it.

I pull hers out too, and something metallic in the bag catches my eye. *Brilliant.* I pull out the large pair of scissors.

Walking back over to her with the edge of the blades tapping against my lower lip, I smile. *This will be perfect.*

I grab a fistful of her hair and yank it. She screeches in pain. Seth likes the sound of her in pain. I hate to admit it, but her screams are kinda growing on me, too.

"If I can't dye it, I'll have to cut it."

Wrenching back her head, I slide the blades near the roots cutting off her locks. The sound of the metal sawing through her coarse hair is empowering. She cries, and I can't help but smile.

You own her now.

Each pile of hair that lands on the ground gives me a rush like I've never felt before. He's right. I *am* in control now. She has to do anything I want.

As I cut, I show no mercy, yanking her head to my will. It's exciting hearing her cry out in pain. Maybe she'll learn not to try and trick me again. I am her master now.

She's yours, Hawk. Yours. You've broken her soul. She'll do whatever you want now.

"No," I whisper. "She'll do whatever *we* want."

Tobias

The road leading to the campus is overgrown with weeds and grasses that have wormed their way through the once-pristine tar. The buildings around it, though abandoned, still cling to the air of greatness they once held.

The Depression hit colleges across the nation pretty hard. People were being laid off; families couldn't make ends met. Students couldn't afford to pay for tuition and employers couldn't swing the higher wages of graduates, so one by one, colleges started folding. It's only now that businesses are starting to recover. Perhaps one day this college will open again, but for now, it's a place of decay and unfulfilled dreams.

A large cast iron gate closing off the main entrance looms before us. When I put my hands on the gate, I expect to feel resistance, but to my shock, it opens. Looking down at the lock, it's clear someone has cut the chains.

"They're here," I whisper.

As I push open the gate, the metal grinds against its rusty hinges, crying out in seeming discomfort. I look over at Kari. She's clutched her hand against her heart, confirming she's just as scared as I am. Together, we walk past the gate and into the unknown.

Our steps are hesitant at first, as though we think Hawk may swoop in and attack us at any moment. But I keep reminding myself that he has no way of knowing we know where he is, so he wouldn't be lurking in the woods, waiting for us.

Gradually, my feet begin to move faster over the cracked pavement, anxious to find their target. *She's here. I can feel her.*

Behind me, Kari struggles to catch up. The sound of her panting chases after me. I probably should slow down so she doesn't have to exert herself, but I can't stop. Not when I'm so close.

The only sounds on the campus seem to be the two of us, yet each step we make thunders against the pavement, potentially giving up our location. My ears strain to pick up anything that might be Jada, but all that registers is the sad cry of the wind. At a large oak tree, I come to a full stop to get my bearings.

"Should we split up?" Kari asks.

"We should, but my damn e-port battery is dead. We'd have no way to stay in contact. Let's just keep walking. I'll be able to sense her if we get close enough." *I hope.*

My eyes rake over the vastness of the campus. It appears to spread out forever. This could take all day!

Kari seems to read my mind. "If he's got her in a frat house, that should narrow our search down. Those are typically placed on the outskirts of the campus," she points out.

Nodding, I set my sites to what looks like the Alumni House. The rest of the campus should be fanned out behind it.

"Okay. So that's where we'll start," I say, pushing my feet toward the brick building that looms large before us, a shadow of the greatness it once commanded.

When we manage to pass the Alumni House, we get our first glimpse of the area we'll need to cover. It's at least several city blocks large. There are cracked roadways that lead in four separate directions. My heart sinks. They could be anywhere.

"We'll find her, Tobias. We'll find her."

As we walk, Kari and I start to figure out how the campus is laid out. The classroom buildings seem to run down the center of the grounds, while the living quarters are sprinkled on either side. Dormitories are mixed in with frat houses, not just on the outskirts like we'd hoped, making the search span over a larger area. We only have a few more houses to check on this end before we'll have to cross over and try the other side. One way or another, however, I'm finding Jada before this day is out. I just hope when I find her, it's not too late. My gut tells me time is not on my side.

Taking a shaky breath, I steal another puff off my inhaler before we start walking again.

CHAPTER SEVENTEEN

Jada

I sit trembling in the chair. My hair is, presumably, all hacked off. I sit and wait for what will happen next.

Across the room, Hawk starts to pace again, gently tapping the blades of the scissors against his bottom lip as he walks. He's looking at me, contemplating.

"I'll buy you a hat."

Tears run down my face as I curse my own vanity. What good is hair now anyway?

Without warning, he throws the scissors across the floor. They skid across the warn floorboards and land under the couch, useless to me. Not that I'd ever be let out of my binds again.

Methodically, he slinks over to the couch and lowers himself onto it, running his hands across his own short, dyed hair.

After a moment, he looks up, but his icy eyes aren't looking at me. I'm not sure they're looking at anything.. Watching him, I witness a glaze form over his eyes. That's when the whispers begin. It's slow at first but then builds to loud and angry bursts of a one-sided conversation.

"...told you... Listen to me... Stop it!... wasting

time… Go get her… No… Do it, Hawk!… risk… He'll be there… Use your knife, stupid."

My mouth goes dry watching the man sitting across from me. His mind is truly not his own. And my life is in his hands.

"Fine!" he shouts so suddenly that it makes me flinch.

Like lightning, he rips himself off the couch and storms past me. He disappears into the second bedroom that I've never seen into. Something slams against a wall before he comes back with a small duffel bag and a stuffed pink elephant. Seeing the toy makes my stomach lurch.

"What are you doing?" I whisper, terrified by his answer.

He stuffs the ball of pink into the bag and flings it over his shoulder.

"I'm going to get our daughter. It's time we start our life." He digs into the bag and pulls out the knife he had earlier, which he slips into his belt with ease.

My heart leaps into my chest.

"No! Please! I'll do anything you want. Anything. Please, please don't touch my daughter."

"*Our* daughter," he seethes, walking to the door. "I'm doing this for us, baby. One day you'll see that."

Great aching sobs come from deep inside my chest as I try to plead with him.

"Hawk, please! Don't do this. She's only a little girl!"

He turns his back to me and straightens his shoulders. "You brought this on yourself, Jada. The time for games is over. You and Janelle are rightfully *mine.* I've waited three years, in *prison,* for this day to come. I'm not waiting any longer. Our new life starts today."

Without another word, he walks to the door, flicks the locks, and marches out, leaving me helpless, alone, and tied to the chair. The sound of the locks clicking back into place causes my body to quake. I thrash against the chair in the off chance I might break it, but it just hops gently off the floor and firmly back in place.

Tobias, please, please don't be at home. Please say you've taken our daughter someplace safe!

Tobias

As we scour the campus, Kari keeps up a constant stream of random chitchat. It's almost as though she's afraid if she stops speaking, she'll lose her grip on reality. My grip left the moment Jada did.

"Tobias, does Jada still... I'm not sure how to put this delicately—"

"No, she doesn't cut anymore," I say, scanning the tree lines.

"Oh, no. Um, I didn't mean that, although I am glad to hear that. I—I just wondered if she was still taking those pills..."

I stop in my tracks. I didn't know Kari knew about those.

"How did you know about that?"

Kari frowns. "By accident. She dropped her bag one day and I saw them."

My eyebrows pinch together, remembering those

days. Before we were together, Jada used to slip some of her dad's prescriptions in order to forget the hell she lived in. It was while she was on those that she slept with Hawk—and got pregnant.

"She hasn't taken those in years," I say.

Kari nods, but I can tell there's something on her mind.

"What is it? What's wrong?"

"It's just—did you know my friend, Naya, was given those same drugs by Seth? He used them to take advantage of her."

I don't mean to be insensitive, but I say, "So?"

"Well, think about it. Jada and Naya both were on that drug. Etash was stabbed in the lung, on the same side you have your ailing lung, and Seth..."

"He shot himself," I say, recalling how he died.

"In the head. Maybe that's how Hawk and Seth are connected. They've both lost their minds—one in the literal sense and one in the figurative sense."

I consider her suggestion and nod slowly.

"Which means we better hurry."

With renewed purpose, we both pick up our pace. After checking the last few houses along the left edge and coming up short, we merge over to the other side of the campus.

My feet tingle as we cross over the grassy hills separating the two sides of the campus. We're getting close.

"This way!" I say, breaking into a run. This was the feeling I'd been waiting for, the "pull" to lead me straight to her.

Just up ahead, a singular frat house is tucked under a

line of willow trees. I stop.

"What's wrong?" Kari asks, coming up beside me.

"Can you smell that?" I whisper. I'm suddenly terrified that my voice might give us away.

Kari looks at me funny, but then smells the air a few times.

"Actually, it kinda smells like Curl Up and Dye."

I turn and give her a confused look.

"My hair salon. You don't think I crawl out of bed looking this gorgeous, do you?" She gives me a wink.

Hair salon... Dye...

"So why would there be the smell of hair dye in an *abandoned* campus?" I say slowly.

I reach around my back and pull out my pistol and unlock the safety.

"Stay here," I tell Kari.

She adjusts her purse and throws her hands onto her hips. "No way in hell."

The look of determination on her face tells me this could be a large battle, and we don't have time to waste.

"Fine, then, stay behind me and keep quiet."

As we creep forward, all my senses are on high alert. Each hair on my body is at attention. The smell of the dye wafts strong with the breeze. The frat house is covered with heavy shadows from the early afternoon sun. The arms of the willow trees almost appear to be hugging the house, cocooning it in a chilly darkness. It's the perfect spot to hide. Just the sort of spot Hawk would snag if he were hunting.

As we're about to move past an overgrown line of shrubs just behind the house, I hear a noise. I yank Kari to the ground behind them and raise my fingers to my lips. She does as told and sinks to the ground without hesitation. She's heard the noise too. Her breathing is labored, and I pray it doesn't give us away. Listening over the thundering of my heart, we stay frozen to our spots.

The sound of a door slamming shut rockets across the campus. Three metallic clicks of locks follow after. Holding my breath, I strain to hear what seems to be only one pair of footfalls crunching along the gravel.

The stride is heavy and long, so I know instantly it's Hawk. Rage bubbles inside of me. I have to fight the urge to spring up from where I'm hiding to take him down, but I wait. I can't risk Jada's safety. I need to make sure she's okay before I hurt Hawk. I'll need him alive if she's not in the house.

The thought of her not being there makes my stomach lurch. *If he's laid a finger on her...*

I hold my breath to see if a second pair of footprints follow, but there seems to be only his. His feet travel quickly. He's in a hurry. For what? I'm about to risk a peek around the shrub when his footsteps suddenly stop. For a solid minute, he doesn't move. I glance at Kari out of the corner of my eye. Her face is locked in fear.

Has he found us? My finger inches silently toward the trigger. If he has discovered us, he'll get the full force of my anger aimed straight at the base of his skull.

Just as I'm about to jump out, the steps begin again. My fingers press firmer on Kari's shoulder as a drip of sweat runs down my face.

Breathlessly, we listen as the sound of a car door opens and closes. It's followed immediately by an engine roaring to life.

"That's *my* car," Kari curses quietly beside me.

We sit in silence as the car backs its way out of the drive and tears off down the main drag, burning rubber.

As if on cue, we both let out the collective breath we've been holding. After making sure the sound of the car dies off, I signal Kari that it's safe to move. Tucking the pistol back in my pants, I stand up.

"Let's go."

The second we're clear of the bushes, I see the faded deep-blue sign:

ΤΚΦ

Tears of relief sting my eyes.

"You found her," Kari whispers.

CHAPTER EIGHTEEN

Tobias

Within seconds, we're at the front of the house. I am prepared to bust down the door like a human battering ram, but I have the foresight to know he wouldn't have left it unlocked.

The first thing I notice is there are black smudges on the chipped brass-painted door handle and two new-looking deadbolts installed above that.

"Jada! Jada! Are you in there?"

I press my head to the door to listen for her. Nothing comes.

To the right of the door there is a window. I rush over to it, picking up a large rock, ready to smash in the thing. My hand stops mid-throw as I notice metal bars have been fashioned across the frame, also new. A quick scan of the house confirms all the windows are barred. I can't even peek inside; he's blacked out all of the windows as well.

That bastard has thought of everything!

I scream her name again as Kari clenches her hands together in fear in a way that seems to say, *Are we too late?*

I go back to the door and shout her name again, trying to drown out all sound but hers.

"Tobias?" The tiniest voice reaches my ears from behind the door, the sound of an angel.

My heart thunders upon hearing her voice. "Jada? Baby! Are you okay? Let me in!"

I can hear her sobbing in relief and it's killing me not to be able to pull her into my arms.

"I can't!" she wails. "He's got me tied up! Tobias, you have to hurry! He's going after Janelle!"

I almost drop to my knees, hearing that blow. I whip around to Kari.

"Call Ms. Skillings. Tell her to bring Janelle to the police station. Now! Get her out of that building!"

Kari scrambles to pull out her e-port as I start thrusting myself at the door. All I end up doing is hurting my shoulder.

I reach for the gun. Locks aren't going to stop me.

"Jada," I yell at the door. "Are you anywhere near the front door?"

"No. I can't reach it, Tobias. Go save Janelle!"

I click the hammer back on the pistol.

"Jada, Janelle is safe. I've got a gun and I'm going to blow the locks off. Are you far enough away?"

"I think so," comes her weak reply.

Swallowing, I aim the gun straight at the bottom lock, close my eyes, and fire. The sound of the shell discharging is deafening amidst the empty campus.

When I open my eyes, I discover I missed. By a long shot. In my head, I can hear Hawk mocking my bad aim.

I fire off another round, this time keeping my eyes

open, but I still miss. Aggravated, I fire one more shot and still don't come close to hitting my target.

Kari grabs the gun from my hands just as I'm about to try again. "You are a pathetic shot."

Pushing me aside, she pulls back the hammer. She points the pistol at the door, squinting slightly, and fires off three rapid shots. The door creaks open at once.

I stare back at her, dazed.

"I know my way around a gun." She shrugs.

"Apparently." She hands me the gun with its one remaining shot, and I tuck it into the back of my pants. "Ms. Skillings is taking her to the police. She'll be safe."

"Thank you."

Now I just need to get Jada the hell out of here before Hawk comes back.

When I kick the door open with my foot, I'm not prepared for what I see.

Jada is sitting slumped over in a kitchen chair. Her hands and feet have been bound. She has large white bandages running along her wrists that have caked over with blood. My stomach rolls. *What has he done to her?*

And her hair… her once-beautiful hair lies in mounds at her feet.

A wave of fury like I've never felt before consumes me. She looks so broken, so weak, worse than she did that night in the hospital when she tried to kill herself. Murderous thoughts run through my mind. That bastard will pay dearly for what he's done to her.

Unable to wait a second longer, I fly over to her side and embrace her shaking body. Her sobs fill my head.

Warm tears land on my shoulder and I curse Hawk's name.

"Shhh, baby. It's okay. I'm gonna get you out of this."

"Tobias," she cries. "I never thought I would see you again!"

We cry together in our awkward embrace before I pull away to look her in the eye.

"Are you hurt?" I ask, inventorying her body. Paying close attention to the bandages along her wrists. "What did he do to you?"

"I'm okay. Just get me out of this, please. We need to get Janelle."

I nod and look over at Kari.

"Can you find something to get her out of this?"

"Under the couch," Jada cries. "He threw a pair of scissors there."

Kari rushes over to the couch and moves it away from the wall. Bending over, she picks up the scissors from their hiding spot and hands them to me. As quickly and as carefully as I can, I cut away the ties around her wrists. The last thing I want to do is hurt her further in my haste to free her. Once the plastic is off her hands, I inspect the damage they made. I carefully pull off the bandages, afraid of what I'll see. Her scars have been sliced open from the ties imprisoning her.

As soon as I release her hands, Jada pulls me into an embrace and sobs hard enough for both of us. The touch of her skin against mine feels so powerful. It's hot, electric burn fills my spirit. I can breathe fully.

"Janelle is fine," Kari says, taking the scissors from me to work on Jada's feet. "Ms. Skillings is bringing her to the police as we speak. All Hawk will find when he gets there is an empty apartment."

"That's good to know," a dark voice says from behind me.

Hawk.

I spin around and reach for my gun, but before I can pull it out, he grabs Kari and holds a sharp blade against her throat. I recognize the style of the knife at once. The tip of it is hooked for organ removal, while the underbelly is honed and lethal. It's a gutting knife.

"Easy now, Tobs. You and I both know what a terrible shot you are. Wouldn't want you killing your friend here instead of me, would you?"

Jada shrinks behind me, clutching onto my sides. Her entire body is trembling.

"Let her go, Hawk," I say, raising my hands slowly into the air. I have to get his knife away from Kari's neck before I make a move. I have to distract him somehow.

"Tsk, tsk, tsk." Hawk taunts. "Six rounds to open one door? I'm offended. Did you learn nothing in our hunting lessons together?"

Six rounds? How did he know how many rounds I used?

"It wasn't very smart of you to make such a racket before I even left the campus. Even if I didn't have impeccable hearing, which I do, a deaf man could have heard your pathetic attempt to shoot a door down."

My teeth grind together in frustration. He's right. That was stupid of me. Of course he would have heard the shots and turned around. Now he's got the upper hand, and he knows it.

"Tell you what," Hawk says. "Since I'm such a nice guy, I'll trade. Jada for Kari." He presses the knife deeper into Kari's neck, causing her to gasp.

"Don't do it," Kari squeaks out.

My fists clench. The gentle squeeze across my waist from Jada reminds me to stay human and not be irrational.

"And then what? You take my daughter away from me too? No way," I spit.

Hawk laughs. "We both know she's not really *your* daughter, now don't we? It's *my* blood that runs through her veins, not yours. And I'll do whatever I want with what is mine."

Every muscle in my body clenches with hatred for the lunatic standing in front of me. No way in hell is that monster going to lay a finger on Janelle.

I'm about to make my move for the gun when Jada beats me to it and makes a move of her own.

Jada

"Stop it!" I shout, stepping out from behind Tobias. "Hawk, if I go with you now, will you promise to leave Janelle alone?"

"What? No!" Tobias screams at me, yanking me back to his chest.

My eyes flick over to Hawk, who appears to be contemplating my proposal.

"Think about it, Hawk." I continue, making the words up as I go. "Bringing Janelle along will only make your plan to disappear even harder. Having her with us would slow us down, and deep down you know it. And now that the police have her, it will be even harder."

Hawks eyes pinch together, but his hands grip the knife tighter. He's gonna go for the trade.

"Jada, what are you doing?" Tobias hisses in my ear. The hurt in his eyes is so strong that I can't bear to look at him anymore. He has to understand. If I could ensure that Janelle was safe, then nothing else mattered. I could take anything Hawk dished out if I knew my baby was with Tobias.

Seeing the determination on my face, Hawk smiles.

"Deal," Hawk says.

"What? No! No deal. I don't agree to this! Jada, what are you saying?" He shakes my arms to get me to look at him, but I just close my eyes. I can't. If I do, my resolve will waiver. I have to do this. I just have to.

"Take care of our daughter," I whisper at the floor. The knots in my throat are so tight that I know I won't be able to say another word without breaking down into a puddle of mush.

"If we're doing this," Hawk says, "we're doing this my way." He tightens his grip on Kari, who has stopped whimpering and is now just staring dead ahead. "The first thing you need to do is get rid of your gun, Tobs."

Beside me, I feel Tobias stiffen with rage. This is the worst situation I ever could have put him in; he has to choose between our little girl and me. He needs to know, in the end, it's the only choice we have.

"Drop the gun, Tobs, or I'll kill the old broad, you, and *still* get Jada." He sinks the knife into Kari's throat.

A small trickle of blood escapes her neck. The look on his face tells me he knows *exactly* how much pressure to put on her vein before it kills her.

Kari gasps against the incision. My eyes flit to Kari, and I catch her give Tobias a small nod.

"Put it on the floor, gently."

I can feel the heat of Tobias's anger as it rolls off his body in waves, but he does as he's told and lowers the gun to the ground.

"Now kick it over here."

Tobias hesitates but then kicks the weapon across the room with remarkable control. The sound of metal sliding against the worn floorboards causes my skin to gooseflesh. It comes to a stop perfectly, just inches from Hawk's feet.

"Good boy," Hawk taunts.

Without taking his grip from Kari or his eyes off of Tobias, Hawk kicks the gun backward toward the door —out of anyone's reach.

"Now, on the count of three, we'll make the switch. And don't think I won't gut the first thing I can get my hands on if you try something funny." His eyes lock with Tobias's in understanding.

"Jada," Tobias whispers. The ache in his voice almost crushes me. Pinching my eyes closed, I steel my nerves for what I'm about to do. I'll have to leave with Hawk, willingly, and never look back. Not even once. My heart would break into a million pieces if I saw Tobias right now.

I can feel my insides already protesting against my decision as every fiber of my being seems to try to pull me backward, toward Tobias. This is going to be the most physically and mentally challenging thing I've ever had to do. But there is no other alternative. I have to do this. I have to do this for my daughter. One day, Tobias will understand. One day, he'll know this was the only choice I could have made.

"One..." The sound of Hawk's countdown shakes me back into the present. "Two..."

I hold my breath and send out into the universe the only thought I have left: *I love you, Tobias. Forever and always.*

Hawk shoves Kari forward a bit in preparation of the switch. Kari's eyes are downcast. Her shoulders are hunched as though she has given up.

"Three."

CHAPTER NINETEEN

Tobias

"Three." The word bounces around in my head like a bad dream. This can't be happening. I can't have gone through all of this to lose her now.

Instinctively, my hand juts out to reach for Jada as her feet inch toward Hawk, but he thwarts my attempt to hold on to her.

"Ah, ah, ah. Let her go, Tobs. I don't want to kill this woman, but I will if you don't get your hands off my girl."

My blood boils, letting him talk to me this way, but he still holds Kari's life in his hands. Kari won't even look at me. It's as though she knows something I don't.

It takes every bit of strength I have in me, but I pry my fingers from Jada's arm, silently whispering my good-byes to her.

The world moves in slow motion as she slips out of my grasp and walks forward. Hawk, looking smug, slowly lowers the knife from Kari's throat by a fraction of an inch.

Jada takes another cautious step toward Hawk, which prompts him to release some of the pressure he has on

Kari's hair.

My heart thunders in my chest. I watch helplessly as Jada takes another step forward. She's within Hawk's grasp now, inches from being taken away from me forever.

That's when the sound of a gun firing and Jada screaming makes us all jump out of our skin.

In front of my eyes, Hawk sinks to his knees. A look of shock is etched across his crazed face. Blood comes pouring out of the side of his neck. Gurgling sounds escape his lips as he grasps at the chunk that is now missing from his throat. His eyes bulge out of his head, looking for the source of the shot.

Hovering over him, Kari aims what looks like a BB gun at him.

"Tobias may be a terrible shot, but I'm not," she tells Hawk.

Kari rounds toward us, keeping Jada and me at her back.

"Tobias, reach into my purse and get my e-port. Call the police. Have them send an ambulance. I think I just nicked his aorta, but if he doesn't get help soon, he'll bleed out."

Stunned, I just stand there for a moment, watching her stand over Hawk.

"Go!" she yells.

Snapping out of my daze, I do as she says. I grab the gadget and start dialing.

"Jada," Kari says, still fully in control, "walk over there and get that gun."

Jada

Like Tobias had, I just stare at Kari, dumfounded. Has she honestly just taken down my captor... with a BB gun?

"I got him covered, Jada. He's not gonna lay a finger on you," she says with so much conviction that it's impossible not to believe her.

With my legs shaking, I make a large arch around Hawk. His limp body crashes to the floor. Dark burgundy blood begins to pool around his head. He's wheezing and moaning, but he is clearly too hurt to stand up.

Still, my legs tremble as I walk around him and approach the gun. I feel like I'm outside myself, not feeling my body move through the space. It's like one bad dream that I can't wake from.

Bending down, I pick up the gun off the ground, surprised by how light it is. Amazing how something so deadly can feel so delicate in my hand.

Carefully, I aim the barrel to the ground and hold it as far away from my body as I can. Circling back, I inch my way over to Kari, terrified I'm gonna trip and end up killing someone with my clumsiness.

When I'm a few steps away, I hold it out to her like it's a dead mouse, not wanting to hold it one second longer, but before I can hand it to her, Hawk's hand juts out suddenly and grabs my ankle. I scream at the feel of his fingers against my flesh. Tobias flies to my side, but I hold out my hand to stop him.

I raise the gun to Hawk's head. "Let. Go. Of. Me."

Tobias freezes at my fierceness.

"Jada, please," Hawk gurgles. "I love you. I just wanted you to love me back..." His voice is so laden with grief that I almost believe him.

Almost.

"I said let go of me." I bring my second hand around the gun to steady my aim.

With a great sigh of defeat, his grasp on my ankle weakens before he finally he releases me and collapses back to the floor.

Tobias rushes to my side and takes the gun from me, shoving me behind him like a human shield. But it's not needed. Instantly, I know the worst is over. The nightmare is over.

Kari switches guns with Tobias, making sure she has the more lethal of the two. Surprisingly, Tobias doesn't seem affronted by the switch at all.

I curl my arms around Tobias from behind and squeeze him tightly, breathing in his earthy scent. *I'm safe.*

"Thank you for finding for me, Tobias."

His free hands curl around mine. I can feel his pulse quicken against my skin upon our contact. He turns to meet my eyes.

"I will always find you, Jada. *Always*. Our souls are bound together forever. Nothing can keep us apart for long. Not even death. No matter what happens to us, I will always find you again."

His words ring deep into my soul. He's right. Leaning against his solid frame, I know with absolute clarity that I will never lose this man again. Even our inevitable deaths will be but a blink of an eye in the grand scheme of things.

I embrace him, closing my eyes, contented. We *will* be pulled back again to each other, no matter how many obstacles try to get in our way. Of that there is no further doubt.

Hawk

Get up off the floor! Stop being so weak! It's just a flesh wound. Get up and claim what's ours!

Opening my eyes, I see Jada wrapped snuggly in Tobias's arms. Where there was rage, there is now only understanding.

Tobias was meant for her. Not me. *Not us, Seth.* It's as clear to me now as the pain coursing in my veins. I have been such a fool.

Blood pools near my eyes, but I can't move away from it. I can't pull my gaze away from my best friend and his girl. They will be happy now.

Just like that, Seth fades away from the corners of my mind and so does the world.

Finally, peace.

CHAPTER TWENTY

Jada

The wedding is set to happen in just a few short minutes and all I can focus on is Janelle's dress. She's managed to spill cranberry juice all down the front of the once-spotless flower girl dress. Her *white* flower girl dress.

Around me is nothing but chaos as people rush to get water, towels, seltzer, anything to try and get the stain out. Only Janelle and I are calm. I know Janelle didn't mean to spill the juice. She's four and still clumsy when it comes to all things liquid. She reminds me of myself at her age.

Still, those around us frantically try to "make it better." They're afraid the day will be ruined now. Nothing could ruin this day. I'm marrying the man of my dreams, and a little juice isn't about to stop that.

Beside me, Kari frowns. Her eyes dart to the clock, then to Janelle.

"Always drama with you, isn't there?" She winks.

I start to laugh as she suddenly pulls the veil from my head.

"Ouch. What are you doing?" I rub at my scalp where she ripped out the bobby pins holding the lace veil that had been, until a moment ago, anchored firmly on my pageboy styled head.

"Oh, you know you hated that veil anyway," she murmurs, pulling out the remaining pins.

It's true. I *did* hate the veil, but that seemed like hardly the point.

With expert ease, Kari wraps the sheer veil around Janelle's dress, draping it in a crisscross pattern—perfectly masking the juice stain. Spinning Janelle around, she ties the ends into an elegant bow. She steps back and admires her work as I stare at her, mouth agape. It's stunning. Absolutely stunning.

The crowd around us stops talking and just stares at the transformation.

"How did you—" I start to say but have no idea how to finish the thought.

Kari just shrugs. "I grew up on the stage. You learn to make do. After all, the show must go on, right?" She gives me a kind grin and gestures to the doorway leading into the church. To Tobias.

Giddy with her new dress, Janelle gives Kari a great big hug, then comes over to tug at my hand.

"Come on, Mama, Papa's waiting."

Tears dance behind my eyes. I rub the growing baby bump and bend over to kiss Janelle.

"You're right, baby girl. Let's go find him."

She picks up her flower basket and runs off ahead of me to take her place up front.

"Thank you, Kari," I choke out when she starts to follow after my daughter.

Kari gives me a small nod, then disappears into the church to take her place as maid of honor.

After a moment, the sound of the music swells and I know it's time. My feet begin moving of their own accord, and I don't resist. I let them pull me back again, toward the only man I'll ever love—in this life and the next.

EPILOGUE

September, 2047

Janelle

The hum of the cafeteria is maddening. You would think the noise buffers plastered overhead would absorb some of the ruckus, but the relentless chatter of pathetic high schoolers abounds, flooding my ears with childish gossip.

One more year, Janelle. You can handle one more year in this hell.

Stabbing my spork into the dehydrated food on my tray, I groan. Although it has all the nutrients I need for the afternoon, I can't stomach this crap today. It tastes like chicken-flavored cardboard. I can wait until I get home and have my parents homegrown potato soup. It's much more appetizing than this mandated mess they call lunch.

Shoving the tray aside, I lean back in my chair and wish the day were over so I could chill out at home. I know it's not cool for a teenager to actually *enjoy* their home, but my folks are kinda awesome, and my brother, Saibot... well, he's annoying, but all little brothers are.

Some could say the same about me, though. I've never been one to bend to people's opinions of what they want me to be. I make waves. Ruffle feathers. Tick people off. So what if I don't have any friends? I don't want them if they think like the rest of these close-minded douche bags.

If it weren't for my folks, I'd probably give up on ever finding a person that actually "gets" me. But because my parents are the most in-love people I know, I figure it's only a matter of time before someone like that turns up to love me the way they love each other. That said, I guess I can handle hanging out in this grotesque purgatory of humanity, knowing soon I won't be alone. Soon my Twin Flame will find me. I just can't see him yet… Sucks, but that's how my visions work. I see snapshots. Bits of time. Not every single moment of the future, just parts my brain thinks I need to know. Not very helpful actually. More of a pain in the ass than anything.

I sigh, waiting for the day to be over. Maybe Ms. Kari will come pick me up and bring me to her new dance studio where I could hang out and dance my butt off. She just opened the studio a month ago, and already she has a huge waiting list to get in with her. She's still got some serious moves for an old lady.

Yawning, I slouch in my chair and take in the view. From my vantage point in the corner of the café (the corner I claimed as my own last year because no one bugs me here), I take in this year's crop of freshman. Each kid that walks in is sadder than the last. All of the freshman are trying to "one-up" the other with this year's fashion or gadget trend. It's pathetic. Don't they realize when they graduate, no one will care? I've seen kids go insane from the pressure to fit in here. And for what? It's just so stupid. Is it any wonder why I sit alone in my corralled-off area and shake my head at all the sheep?

A freshman boy starts to head my way, probably not seeing that I've already claimed this spot. For a moment, he looks hopeful. Then as he gets nearer, a light goes off in his head, like he's just now figured out who I am. He stops mid-stride, then turns around and away from me as fast as his feet can carry him.

I can't help but laugh. I tend to scare people away just because I can see into the future. You'd think they'd *want* to know what their fate was. Oh well, their loss. I wish I could tell how *my* fate was gonna work out, but it doesn't seem to work that way. At least I know my folks are gonna be with me for a long time, even if they don't want me to tell them their future.

I'm itching to tell them that Ma's about to write a book about her life that's gonna make us millionaires, but they hate to know what's coming up, so I just sit with that little gem in the back of my head and plan out the designs I'm gonna have for my new room once the book drops next year.

From the corner of my eye, the one I've been having visions of for weeks walks in. I think her name is Jenevra? She looks as scared as a drowning rat. Her hands are trembling slightly against her tray as she scans the room for a place she can disappear into. Poor thing. She hasn't been "claimed" yet by any of the other cliques. That's just 'cause they don't know what to make of her. She lost her parents in a car crash just before summer was over, so no one knows how to talk to her.

I can relate, well, sort of. I've lost a parent too. My biological dad died when I was only three, but I can't be sad. I never really knew him, and besides, his lung saved my father's life. From what little they tell me about him, he wasn't well-liked. They hardly ever talk about him. It's times like that I wish I could see the past.

Focusing back on the girl, I notice she has jet-black hair, like, so dark it looks like someone dropped a bottle of ink on her head. And she's pale, white-bread pale. Her whole aura is crying out to be swallowed up by any of the groups around her, anyone to reach out a friendly hand and take her in. Tragic. No self-confidence.

Someone shouts her name from across the room and I glance up. My eyes follow to where she looks. *Ugh!* It's Hunter Walsh. I frown. He's a sophomore and a prick with a capitol P. Every girl he's ever dated has ended up with strange-looking bruises that look oddly like his fingerprints all over their arms. But he's super popular, so the girls keep coming to him.

I look back to my wet rat. The hesitation in her eyes is obvious. She doesn't want to go to his table. She can sense he's trouble, but she doesn't know what else to do. She's weak. Vulnerable. Just the sort of woman a guy like Hunter could sink his talons into.

Of course, I have no choice. I have to save her.

"Jenevra!" I shout, standing up. "Over here."

She meets my gaze. A thick wave of relief floods over her. Her dark-blue eyes flick back and forth between the two tables—hesitating.

Make the right choice. My eyes burn into hers. *I have much to tell you about your future.*

She rocks against the balls of her feet for a moment, unaware of the gravity of the choice she makes in this moment.

I hold my breath as her feet push forward and away from Hunter, unknowingly breaking any hold he may have had on her life.

I break out into the only real smile I've ever had at school. The best friend I'd been waiting for pulls up a seat next to me.

Life is just about to get good.

THE END

Danielle Bannister is a work at home mom of two small children living in rural Maine. She has her BA in theatre and her Masters in Literary Education and working hard on several other novels. She has written the first in this trilogy, *Pulled*, as well as a collection of short works entitled *Short Shorts*. Her work can also be found in the 2012 edition of The Goose River Press Anthology and the 2012 Maine Writing Project's Anthology, *Writeous*. She has also written *Pulled, Pulled Back and Pulled Back Again.*

She has a new novel, *The ABC's of Dee* coming out in April 2015

You can follow her writing struggles on her website at: http://daniellebannister.wordpress.com/or find her on Facebook at: www.facebook.com/BannisterBooks

Or Tweet her @dbannisterbooks

or e-mail her at: daniellebannisterbooks@gmail.com

BOOK CLUB QUESTIONS

1. All three novels focus on the idea of Twin Flames. Do you believe they exist? Have you ever witnessed a Twin Flame?

2. In the novels, the main characters struggle with self-worth. Has there ever been a time where you've had such struggles?

3. Abuse is a major theme in all three novels—physical, emotional, and self-inflicted. Why do you think so many turn to violence as an answer to their troubles?

4. Some of the characters in this series can see into the future. Would you consider that to be a gift or a curse?

5. What would you do if you met your Twin Flame on the side of the road?

6. Is there any burning question you want the author to answer for you? Feel free to e-mail her at daniellebannisterbooks@gmail.com